"Phoenix,"

said the Lady of the Bees,

"I'm going to live for a long time. When you're an old, old man and your father is dead, I'll still be much as you see me now. That city he's going to build—it may not be the one. The Second Troy, I mean, predestined by the gods. But in time there will be such a city, and somehow I think I'm going to be there to see it built. Who knows, I may help to consecrate the ground or lay the first stone!

"Anyway, I'll be keeping a watchful eye on your great-great-great grand-children, and I can tell you now that they need never fear the forest, neither lions nor vengeful queens."

But where lions and vengeful queens were concerned, not even a green-haired non-human can always predict right . . . as Phoenix was to find out.

GREEN PHOENIX

by
Thomas Burnett Swann

Illustrated by
GEORGE BARR

DAW BOOKS, INC.
DONALD A. WOLLHEIM, PUBLISHER

1301 Avenue of the Americas
New York, N. Y.   10019

FIRST PRINTING, OCTOBER 1972

3 4 5 6 7 8 9

Part One

CHAPTER I

"Aeneas must die."

The words were both a command and a covenant. Aeneas, the Trojan butcher, betrayer of women, invader of the Wanderwood, must die, and she, Mellonia, the Dryad, seventeen years of age, who wept when she crushed a bee or broke a spider's web, was bound by the oath as surely as her queen, Volumna. Unless the stories told of Aeneas were lies—and their truth was attested by warriors, mariners, and Amazons—she must obey the oath and, if it fell to her lot, murder the murderer for the safety of her people and the sanctity of the forest.

Now it was night. That same afternoon, when the sun had sat in the treetops like a nesting phoenix, Aeneas had seemed no more to her than a name whispered to frighten a naughty child.

Her hive had been ravaged by a hungry bear. The bear had not enjoyed his feast; he had been stung into a hasty flight through blackberry brambles and into the soothing waters of the Tiber. Still, the hive was in ruins, the bees were honeyless and homeless, and she had located a new stump for them within sight of the tree where she had lived for a year, alone, sometimes lonely, but companioned by her bees and her animals, since the death of her mother in a thunderbolt. Now she was showing the stump to the queen. The bees could understand Mellonia's gestures but few of her words; she could understand their flight patterns but

7

few of their buzzings. It was poor communication but better than none, and the queen, by her rapid zigzags, was certainly expressing gratitude. Mellonia's favorite, a drone whom she called by the name of Bonus Eventus or Good Luck, had alighted on her shoulder to rest.

Her friend, Bounder, the Centaur, cantered out of the woods and circled Mellonia and the stump. In the fashion of his race, who inclined to the foppish and basked in admiration, he smote the earth with his hooves and shook his mane as if it were wheat in the wind. At first she chose to ignore him; she did not like his stares, which had lately become more frequent and assertive, almost as if her ears had lost their points or her green hair had escaped from its fillet. She belonged to that tribe of Dryads known as Oakarians, who had no need for men, so they claimed, and little liking for them. They were the Dryads who conceived without fertilization from any males. While her friends remained in another part of the forest, a Dryad of childbearing years would conceal herself in the Sacred Oak of Ruminus; drink of the holy beverage distilled from poppy heads, sleep a dreamful and sometimes disturbing sleep, and awake, if she were fortunate, with life in her womb.

But Mellonia liked Bounder; he was young and parentless and, though at seventeen she was a mere stripling when the average life span of a Dryad was that of her oak—possibly as long as five hundred years—she liked to mother him. In fact the other Dryads often teased her that she had no need to enter the Sacred Oak; she was already mother to half the forest-bees, fawns, Faun kids, wolf cubs—the list would have filled a large clay tablet. Thus, in spite of his disconcerting stares, she turned from the grateful, graceful gyrations of the queen and smiled to Bounder.

"All that trouble over a hive of bees," he grumbled. A Centaur's voice was deep, melodious, cultivated, and altogether agreeable to her ears. The celebrated travels of the race had made them eloquent if also a little vain.

"I like their honey."

"If they made wolfsbane, you would still like them. You like everything."

"No," she was quick to correct him. "Only kind

8

things. Growing things. Some things I hate." It was true; on her arm she still bore the tooth marks of a lion who had killed a Dryad baby when Mellonia was fourteen. She had followed the killer to his lair, taken him by surprise—for Dryads smelled like oak trees and walked as silently as deer—and killed him with a club and without compunction. Bounder, doubtless remembering the incident, retreated a few paces, almost stumbling over his hooves.

"You're right," he admitted. "But don't look at me that way. I'm not a lion."

"I've found them a new home," she explained about the bees. "That clumsy bear—"

"One of the bees is crawling between your breasts."

"He's a drone. They don't like to work."

"I envy him."

"And what work did you ever do except comb your mane?"

"I meant I envied his position." Centaurs were fond of breasts; in fact, they seemed to prefer humans or Dryads to their own women for that particular appurtenance; but Mellonia had been taught that a breast served no other function than to give suck, and Bounder's interest puzzled her.

"Speaking of work, I've brought a message for you," he continued.

"What is it?"

Bounder was young and exquisitely groomed, since the agricultural Centaurs paid the Fauns with vegetables from their gardens to do their menial chores—sweep their triangular, timber-built huts and repair the thorn-topped walls which enclosed their village—and thus had time in which to exercise and groom themselves. Furthermore, they prided themselves on the grace and range of their conversation. Bounder's flanks and his multiple appendages—four legs and two arms—were lithe and tawny; he kept himself immaculate by bathing in the Tiber. His face, if one liked masculine faces, was pleasingly symmetrical, the gold eyes luminous in the rosy, beardless skin, the mane a little golden garden running profusely from his head down the back of his neck.

She smiled indulgently. "Bounder, in some ways

9

you're still a colt." The only kisses she knew were the chaste exchanges between Dryads. She kissed him lightly on the cheek as she had often and affectionately kissed her mother.

"Now it's my turn."

"I kissed you. I didn't say you could kiss me back."

"It doesn't hurt, you know."

Stiffly she proffered her cheek. Such foolishness! The marjoram scent of his breath was not unpleasant as his lips approached her, but suddenly he bypassed her cheek and seized upon her mouth. She began to burn— not only her mouth, but all of her—with a curious and not entirely unpleasant fire. By the milk of Rumina, was he trying to suffocate her. And here were his arms encircling her like the necks of a Hydra!

She wrenched free of him. Centaurs, though swift runners in an open field, were laughably awkward at close range.

"If you don't give me the message, I'll give you fifty bee stings," she said, raising a hand as if she were about to arouse the hive against him.

"Oh, very well," he said, trying to sound casual but looking anxiously at the bees. "Will you comb my mane first? The wind has tousled it." He drew a tortoiseshell comb from the lionskin bag he wore around his neck.

"And you promise not to kiss me again?"

"I promise. Today."

"Ever."

"Ever." It was almost a sigh.

She ran the comb through his mane, though not a hair seemed out of place. He had stiffened it with a mixture of resin and myrrh. Then, she gave a sisterly pat to his flank and felt an unexpected twitch.

"How pretty you've grown! Like a hyacinth."

Pretty? Flowers were pretty. Swallows. Butterflies. Varicolored stones on the bottom of a stream. But no one had ever applied the word to her. She resisted the urge to ask him, "How am I pretty? Do you like the green of my hair? It isn't perfect, you know. There are golden streaks from the sun—"

Quickly she withdrew her hand and said: "And how about the message?"

10

"Volumna has called a meeting beneath the fig tree of Rumina."

"What about?" Mellonia gasped. Such meetings were rare. They indicated decisions of a momentous nature.

"Danger, I should think."

"What sort of danger?"

"I don't know," he said, and Mellonia believed him. Momentous affairs were not discussed with males, much less Centaur males; it was enough to entrust them with messages.

Already she was hurrying toward the fig tree, the Ficus Ruminalis, half a mile from her home. She wore neither boots nor sandals nor heavy robes, but anklets of red berries, and a tunic of green linen which twinkled like leaves in the sun, and a necklace of green acorns, and it would have taken a deer to overtake her. Certainly not Bounder, unless they had been on clear and level ground. She felt him staring after her as she outdistanced him, and wondered why he had quivered when she touched him. And all his talk about kisses! Why, they had grown up together! He was the one male her mother had tolerated around the tree.

But expectation of the assembly, of the danger, effaced all thoughts of him. . . .

The tree was large for its kind and freighted with small green kernels, soon to ripen into figs which no bee would dare to assault unless it fell to the ground. There was an understanding between the bees and the Dryads, for the tree was Goddess and Mother, the figs were her children. So were the Dryads.

It was half an hour's walk to the oak of conception, the oak of Ruminus, divine consort to Rumina though decidedly the lesser deity and therefore consigned to a less desirable part of the Wanderwood.

The council chamber was an artificial cave under the fig tree. Rootlets dangled from the roof like arriving snakes, but the Dryads had dug deeply and carefully so as not to cut the larger roots, the arteries of their mother.

Resin torches, recessed in the earthen walls, burned steadily in the windless air; wooden benches rose in semicircular tiers, a design which, devised by the

Dryads on Crete in a time beyond remembering, had inspired the Cretans to build arenas for their bull games. There were perhaps fifty Dryads, adults and children, in the chamber, all of them female. If a Dryad gave birth to a boy, she promptly exposed him to the forest. If the lions did not get him, perhaps a kindly Centaur mother would rear him along with her own young, or a Faun—and all Fauns were male—would permit him to live with his scraggly, odorous, and happy brood. It was such a boy that Mellonia, at the age of fourteen, had rescued with the thought of rearing him as a brother, but her mother had quickly returned him to the place of his exposure. "It is Rumina's Law," she had said. The next morning Mellonia had found the telltale tracks of a lion, the same beast which she had summarily dispatched with her club. She had not spoken to her mother for a week. In the end it was her mother who had made peace between them by allowing her to make friends with Bounder.

"Aeneas has landed at the mouth of the Tiber." All of the Dryads were small, a mere four feet or so in height, but Volumna gave the illusion of size. It was her straight carriage, her strong, resonant voice, which rang like a conch shell, her green hair raised above her head with copper pins, her pointed ears, bared and sharp and looking rather like the fir-wood darts which the Fauns used in their blowguns, against the lions. Mellonia respected her; she almost succeeded in loving her.

"Aeneas has landed. . . ." That was all; it was not necessary to say more. Even the very young knew that the best of males was to be tolerated only for purposes of trade or carrying messages or joining in common defense against invaders of the Wanderwood, and that the worst of males was Aeneas. Everyone knew his story; perhaps fifteen years ago—the exact number depended on the teller—he had forsaken his wife in the flames of stricken Troy, preferring to rescue his small son, Ascanius, and his aged father, a wretched old liar who claimed to have lain with the goddess Venus. After many wanderings, he had landed in Carthage, accepted the hospitality of its queen, Dido, seduced her into marriage to gain supplies for his ships, and callously

12

forsaken her. She had died by her own hand on a funeral pyre and her vengeful sister Anna had followed him to Italia (where he was bound, so he had said, at the prompting of the gods) in order to spread the word of his sins. Now, after many wanderings and no doubt many seductions, for in spite of his middle years he was said to be attractive to women, he had landed where the Tiber met the sea, a few miles from the grove of the Oakarians.

"He is a man," muttered Mellonia's aunt, Segeta, "and what is more he is human." There were humans who lived on the borders of the Wanderwood, the Volsci, but at least they were ruled by a woman, Camilla, and they did not disturb the Wanderwooders—Fauns, Dryads, Centaurs, and the rest. But foreigners—roads—cities—wars. Worst of all, *men*. Such things were unspeakable; unthinkable.

"Our trees will be cut to build their galleys and their forts."

"And we," said Volumna, "will become their spoils."

"Spoils? I don't understand," said Mellonia. Her mother had died before she could tell her the full range of male iniquity.

"They will take us into their huts."

"We will be their slaves?"

"Worse."

"They will kiss us? On the mouth?"

"They will make us bear their children."

"As if we had lain in the Sacred Tree?"

"We must lie with *them*. Like the animals."

Mellonia had raised enough sheep and deer to know that they coupled before they bore offspring. The Centaurs were too fastidious to make love in public, but the Fauns, naked and shameless, thought nothing of copulating in the shade of a Dryad tree. Mellonia had pelted one such couple with acorns and received a derisive invitation from the male, Mischief by name, to replace his present partner. The incident had both humiliated and sickened her. She also knew that some Dryads were forced to couple with males. Those to the far north, for want of a sacred oak, took husbands among the Fauns. But a *human* male. There would be kisses, mouth to mouth. And worse. It would be a violation and a

13

degradation. It would be as if her tree were consumed by flames. (A wicked thought invaded her brain, like a bee invading a fig: Not every fire consumes. A little heat is a kindly thing—a brazier in the late fall, before the White Sleep; an open fire in the woods.)

She remembered Aeneas and forced a considerable shudder.

"Of course he must die," said Volumna.

"Of course," said Segeta.

"Of course," echoed the other, older women. Their faces shone like daisies in the dim light; their voices were myrrh; but their words dripped like the deadly sap of the oleander. The children nodded their heads in mute, fascinated approval.

"Perhaps he will sail away," suggested Mellonia. "There is nothing for him here." She did not want to kill, whether the victim was Wanderwooder, animal, or human, unless he was cruel like the lion, and the thought of killing Aeneas disturbed her only less than the thought of enduring his embraces. She had heard much to arouse her against him; she was almost ready to believe and condemn; but first she must see the tangible proof of his perfidies.

"He has moored his ships in the mouth of the Tiber. His men are scouting the region for a place in which to build a town. And of course they want women. There are a few Trojan women with them, but the years have not been kind to them. They want young girls like you."

"But if he is a great warrior, and men cannot kill him, what can we do?"

"Ah, but you see he will be on guard against men. Fauns or Centaurs cannot get close to him. Even if they could, what are slings against swords? But women—he preens himself on his power over them. He expects them to wilt into his arms. We shall do exactly that—whichever of us encounters him first. And when he removes his armor—"

"I've never killed a man," said Mellonia.

"You've killed a lion," said Volumna. "It is much the same thing. Except that Aeneas is more dangerous, because he is more clever."

"What does he look like?"

14

"The Faun who spied the landing—it was Mischief, as you might suppose—did not say. He was afraid to be seen. I would expect Aeneas to look like any Trojan warrior. Brutish and hawk-eyed. Hair on his face as sharp as brambles. Arms like oaken clubs. And old, I should think. Fifteen years of wanderings must have left their toll."

"I have heard that he was only about twenty-five when he left Troy, and Dido found him irresistible."

"It was five years ago when he landed in Carthage, and Dido was widowed and easily charmed. Forty is young to us, but to a warrior who fought at Troy, to a sailor whom Neptune's storms have tossed and buffeted, it is venerable old age. I expect you will find him as weathered as my oak."

Volumna stared solemnly at the assembly. "Join hands, my sisters. Repeat after me:

" 'Here beneath the Sacred Fig Tree of life, we swear to kill the man who invades our land with death. A warrior he comes, and warriors we greet him, we who love spring and the budding bough and the building bird; we who can wield a club and face the fiercest lion, the breaker of boughs, the despoiler of nests.' " She removed a pin from her hair, a copper bee with a long stinger, and calmly pierced her arm. She passed the pin to the Dryad beside her, and after it a small silver urn in the shape of a hive, and each woman and child—Mellonia in turn—pierced her skin and drew green blood and filled and returned the cup to Volumna.

"Sylvanus, god of nightmares, killer of fawn and rabbit, we invoke your terrors against our common enemy. This is Aeneas' blood." Then, upturning the cup:

"Thus, Aeneas."

"This is Aeneas' blood!"

CHAPTER II

Smokily silver, under the moss-laden boughs of oak trees older than Saturn, the Tiber flowed toward the Trojan ships and the sea. Ascanius lay on the bank and watched Aeneas, his father, splash in the water with Delphus, the dolphin who had followed them from Sicily. Aeneas and Delphus were playing a game with a wooden stick. Aeneas would throw the stick, Delphus would erupt under it and hurl it back to him with his elongated snout and then make a noise with his airhole or his mouth—Ascanius was not sure which—uncannily resembling a human laugh.

Betrayed cities, suicidal queens, tempests at sea, fifteen years of wandering ... Thrace ... Delos ... Crete ... Carthage ... Italia. But now Aeneas was laughing like Delphus; forgetting, it seemed, the grief and the guilt which hounded him like the Furies. Silver-haired Aeneas with the face of a young man. When you saw the back of his head, you might think him old because of his hair. When he turned to face you, he might have been twenty-five, the blue eyes clear and gently penetrating, the teeth white and perfect, the ruddy cheeks beardless, unlined, and unscarred except for a tiny cleft in his chin (a gift from Achilles' ax). But then, so the stories ran, Aeneas' mother had been the goddess Aphrodite, or Venus as she was called in Italia. Immortal mother, mortal father; youth and age in the same god-man. Perhaps it was a lie; perhaps his mother had been a serving maid. Never mind, he was

17

still Aeneas, more than a man; to Ascanius, more than a god.

"Aren't you going to swim anymore?" Aeneas shouted.

"I'm tired. I've crossed the river three times already!"

"Why not four?"

"Because I'm not Aeneas. Come and sit with your indolent son."

Aeneas parted the reeds on the river bank and stood tall in the sunlight; tall, at least, for a Dardanian-turned-Trojan, though beside Achilles he would have looked like Harpocrates, the child-god of the Egyptians. Ascanius looked quickly at the oak trees behind them and the loincloths, quivers, and bows beside them. A seasoned warrior in spite of his youth, he had heartily disapproved of leaving their ships and friends and armor at the mouth of the Tiber, in a strange land known for its barbarous men and its men like beasts. But Aeneas had been like a child planning a picnic—honey cakes to eat, berries to pick—in the world's great childhood before the Trojan War.

"We'll explore together, and then we'll swim in the Tiber and lie in the sun! And hunt for game as we return to the ships."

"And find a net thrown over us or a spear in our hearts. You saw that Satyr skulking in the woods. He's probably alerted the whole forest. It was bad enough that time we fought the Harpies. And they were only women with wings and claws. I'm not going to lose my father to an odorous goat man."

"If we go together, Phoenix, we can look after each other." "Phoenix" was Aeneas' special name for him. ("Ascanius is too long and As is too undignified.") "Or must I go alone?"

Of course Ascanius had joined him. Aeneas always got his way; he rarely gave commands, he gave invitations, and people accepted, less because he was a king than because he was that rarity among men, gentleness without weakness, strength without cruelty, a fighter who was also a poet; in short, a practical dreamer.

Now they lay in the sun while Delphus dozed on the river in the fitful fashion of dolphins, almost sinking

18

below the surface, rising to open his eyes and look for sharks or mischievous Tritons.

"Will we build at the mouth of the Tiber?"

"Inland, I should think. Protected from Carthaginian galleys. First we must meet Latinus and buy or borrow some land." Latinus was the strongest king in an area known as Latium; area, not country, for the few cities were small, independent, and separated by almost impenetrable forests. "And don't forget the prophecy that we must build where we find a white sow and thirty piglets. But now, let's lie in the sun and not look for pigs."

Only in repose did Aeneas' face look sad, and all the sadder because it looked so young. His body was quiet, the tautness gone from the muscles, but his eyes were open and staring, it seemed, at the flames of Troy, at his wife, Creusa, Ascanius' mother, as she fell behind him in the crowd while he carried his aged father on his shoulders and held Ascanius, five years old, by the hand. He had stopped to look for her.

"No!" Creusa had cried above the tumult, the axes hacking at wooden columns, the hiss of flames as they bit into halls and temples. "I'll catch up with you. Get our son to the ships." They had never seen her again. . . .

Ascanius tried to discourage what he called the "remembering moods" in his father. He had killed a man for saying that Aeneas had forsaken his wife. He would kill any man—or woman—who insulted or threatened him; he would die the death of Hector to spare him pain.

He pressed his father's hand. "I'm happy today," he said. Unlike the cool, conquering Hellenes, the Dardanians were an affectionate and demonstrative people. The men honored their wives as equals; fathers and sons embraced without embarrassment. When Dardania fell to the Hellenes and her surviving warriors went to fight with embattled Troy, they came to be called "the gentle killers." Fortunate were their friends, the Trojans, but Zeus preserve their enemies!

"Why, Phoenix?"

"Because we came. Just the two of us. You can rest from being a legend and I can look after you."

19

"Legend!" laughed Aeneas. "Demon, the Carthaginians would say. Or the Hellenes."

"That's true. But to your men—to anyone who really knows you—a great hero. Either way, a legend, and don't deny it. Is there any land on all the shores of the Great Green Sea that hasn't heard of Aeneas and his wanderings and his dream of rebuilding Troy in a foreign land? Why, you're as famous as Odysseus!"

"At least he got home," Aeneas said wistfully, "and I'm still wandering. But then, he had to wander alone, while I have my son."

"Do you know what I think, Father? It's true you're a legend, but locked inside is—"

"What?"

"A happy little boy. The one you never had time to be. Almost as soon as Grandfather brought you back from that mysterious expedition of his where he met Grandmother—you must have been six months old— they started to train you to be a prince or a king. But the little boy is still inside of you, and every now and then he slips out and plays fetch and carry with a dolphin—and then I feel like *his* father. If the gods gave me one wish, it would be: Set the little boy free. Stop driving Aeneas to lead men and build cities. Let him throw the discus and swim in the Tiber and never grow up or old, and give him a brother—me!"

"And this is my wish. Let me build my city, my second Troy, but only if Ascanius consecrates the ground."

"You'll get that wish."

"Whisper, Phoenix. Some of the gods are jealous. Poseidon or Hera may overhear you."

"Never mind. They can't hurt you now. Isn't Aphrodite your mother? What will you do when you've built your city?"

"Give you the throne and retire to compose an epic."

"About your wanderings?"

"About Hector. He was the great one, you know. Achilles was stronger in battle, but Hector knew how to love."

"You always wanted to be a bard, didn't you? But the gods made you fight an epic instead of write one."

"There's still time for both, I hope." Then, without

20

lowering his voice, "I hear something in the woods, Phoenix. When I give the signal, jump to your feet and grab your bow. . . . *Now!*"

Quick as the bird for which Ascanius was named, the two men were standing and armed, though still naked and glistening from their swim in the Tiber. They looked toward the forest, ready to fire at beasts or flee from armored men. A young woman—or was she a goddess?—stood at the edge of the trees, looking at them with uncertainty but without fear. There was something insubstantial about her, as if the Great Mother had dreamed her out of sunlight and mist.

She spoke the Latin tongue which Aeneas and Ascanius had learned in Carthage, a city sometimes visited by merchants from the ports of Italia.

"You must be Aeneas' men." Her voice did not dispel the illusion of her unreality; it was like the song of a nightingale, but without its wounding sadness.

"Is she my grandmother?" Ascanius whispered.

"No, she's only a girl. Aphrodite is ageless. But she might be Hebe or Iris."

"Yes, we're his men," said Ascanius loudly. "Our names are Phoenix and—Halcyon. Aeneas is with the ships."

"When I first saw you," she said to Aeneas, "I thought you might be Aeneas himself. Your back was turned to me in the river and I only saw your silver hair. It seemed to speak of years and wanderings. But once I saw your face, I knew that you and your companion were brothers. Phoenix and Halcyon. The bird of life and the bird of peace."

"Why did you want Aeneas?" Ascanius asked. He did not trust this girl. She was surely no Amazon like the Volscian queen, Camilla, who had sworn to kill Aeneas because of her people's alliance with Carthage. But there were women who conquered through wiles instead of weapons. There had been a woman named Helen.

"To greet him," she said. Then, quickly (too quickly, it seemed to Ascanius), "I never saw naked men before. The Volscian men wear tunics or armor. Even if they didn't they wouldn't be much to see. It's their women who rule, you know. Of course I've seen Fauns,

21

but they're more goat than man. I have always been told that men were almost as disgusting. Bristling hairs and smudges of dirt all over them. But I think you are very pretty, both of you. Is that a word for men? Much prettier than women. I mean, I like the bronze of your skin, the hard muscles." She pointed to her breasts. "I suppose you might call me misshapen. I bulge where you are flat."

Ascanius laughed. "It depends on the point of view." She walked toward them.

"Aren't you afraid of us?" Ascanius asked.

"Why should I be?"

"We're warriors. You're a woman, and unprotected."

"Do I need protection from you?"

"From me you do!" He was deeply stirred by this miracle of young womanliness, though he continued to mistrust her. Like most warriors, he had sometimes taken a woman after capturing a city, and several cities had fallen to Aeneas and his exiled Trojans. There was no pleasure to equal possessing a woman who made a show of resistance but knew when to yield. Ascanius had lost track of the women he had possessed since his first conquest at the rather advanced age of fifteen, some of them willing at the start, some protesting, all of them satisfied at the conclusion. In the cities of Hellas— Tiryns, Mycenae, Athens—even in gentler Troy and Dardania, rape was as often a compliment as an affront, and it was only a crime when committed in a temple, like Ajax's rape of Cassandra. Zeus himself had set enough examples.

"Do you mean you might kill me?"

"Oh no. What a waste that would be!"

"I suppose you mean, then, that you might kiss me, and—what is the word?—spoil me."

"Not spoil you, *make* you a spoil."

"It sounds to me like much the same thing. I've been kissed once already, and if what follows is more energetic, well, I should be quite spoiled."

"It depends on the spoiler. I would be very careful."

Calmly she drew a copper pin from her upswept hair. It was very sharp, with a hilt like a bee. A tiny sword. "I could stab one of you and outrun the other. I defy any Trojan to outrun me."

"You won't need your little weapon on us," said Aeneas. "If you will turn your back, we will get into our loincloths."

"I never turn my back on strangers," she said. "It is either ill-mannered or unsafe. Besides, I've already seen whatever there is to see, haven't I? When you get your clothes on, will you talk with me a little?"

She sat on a mossy rock and smiled at both of them, though perhaps a little more at Aeneas. The green hair, becomingly streaked with gold, the pointed ears, the diminutive stature—a Dryad, what else? Fled for centuries from the eastern end of the Great Green Sea—fled too from Crete, the island shaped like a ship—but here they endured and indeed seemed to flourish, if not to rule.

"Is your animal friendly? His eye has a crafty gleam. I haven't much acquaintance with dolphins. They don't often swim up the Tiber and I seldom go to the sea. It's too far from my oak."

"He's generally harmless," said Ascanius. "Except to those who would harm my—brother—and me." He still did not altogether trust her, and he trusted her the less because the stirring he felt was new to him and compounded of something more than mere desire, though certainly, fervently he desired her. In one way or another, he felt that she was a menace.

"I have a friend too. See?" She pointed to a bee circling lazily above her. "I call him Bonus Eventus because he brings me luck. Of course he's a drone and can't sting. But he carries messages. Now tell me about your leader. We have heard tales of him even here. But tales are sometimes altered in the telling. We have heard that he helped to betray his city to the Hellenes and then forsook his wife in the flames."

Ascanius' voice turned bronze. "You have heard lies. The story of his treachery was invented by those who envied his prowess. Aeneas is a great hero. Furthermore, he was a devoted husband to Creusa. He left her only in order to get his small son and his lame father to the Trojan ships on the beach. Then he returned to search for her. He never found her. She was a sweet and radiant lady and he never ceased to mourn."

She looked at him with eyes as green as young acorns. "I believe you are telling me the truth as you know it. But you were a small child at the time, Phoenix." It was both flattering and unsettling to have her use his father's pet name for him on so short acquaintance. "How can you know what truly happened?"

"Believe me, I know."

"And Dido? Did he not forsake her?"

"He obeyed the command of the gods and departed from Carthage to rebuild Troy. He asked her to come with him. She refused."

"And killed herself out of love for him?"

"Out of wounded pride and self-pity." Ascanius had never liked the queen of Carthage. Her dark rages, her feverish laughter, even her dusky loveliness had repelled him. She had made him think of a panther.

"No," said Aeneas gently. "I think she truly loved him. But she could not leave her people, and when he was gone, she could not stay with them either. She was a troubled woman; she had known too many losses. As for Aeneas, he loved her next to Creusa and his son. He still grieves for her and prays that her wandering shade may have found its peace in Elysium."

She shook her head in bewilderment. A curl escaped from her upswept hair and tumbled over her ear. He wanted to sweep it back into place. He liked her pointed ears. Their tips looked as soft as antelope fur.

"It all sounds so different, coming from you. It isn't the way I've heard it at all. I must see him for myself. If he is truly kind, why then—"

"He is the kindest man I have ever known," said Ascanius with ardor.

"You love him because he is your leader. I love Volumna, my queen. Even if they erred, we might not see their faults. Thank you, Phoenix and Halcyon. Now I must go."

"But what is your name?" cried Ascanius.

"Mellonia."

"The Lady of the Bees," said Aeneas. "Do you live on honey?"

"Yes," she laughed, "and I have a stinger. But not

24

for you and your brother. Especially not for you. You're very quiet, but I think I like your thoughts." Then she was gone, and with her, Bonus Eventus.

"She's much too beautiful to be so trusting," said Ascanius. ("Or to trust," he muttered under his breath.) "We could have taken her, you know. In spite of her weapon."

Aeneas stared after her.

"You *were* very quiet with her, Father. Now you're quiet with me. What are you thinking?"

"That she somehow looked like your mother."

"You see Mother's face in every beautiful woman. I saw the prettiest bedmate this side of Olympus."

"Phoenix, no harm must ever come to that girl."

"Father, I don't intend to hurt her. Don't you think that women like to be bedded? Don't you know that every woman aboard our ships would like to be bedded by you? As for me, am I so ill-favored and gross?"

Aeneas embraced him with a hearty laugh. It was good to hear his laugh; to feel it rumbling in his chest; deep and manly and yet somehow too a child's laugh, welling spontaneously out of a secret place in him which sorrow had never reached; where magic was everyday and gods walked with men instead of fought with them. "Uncomely? Even Dido had eyes for you, and you were only fifteen at the time. Why do you suppose I call you Phoenix?"

"Because of my yellow hair." Most Dardanians were dark, but Aeneas' hair had been gold before it turned silver the night when Troy fell, and Phoenix's hair was the same rich color. "Aphrodite's gold," people said.

"Also because so many women are burned by your fire!"

"I have to make up for my father, who is first in battle but last in bed. Who has only lain with two women in his whole life, and both of them his wives. Why, it's downright scandalous."

"I leave the burning to you. But not Mellonia. I'm sure she's a virgin. Lying with her would be a violation. Except in marriage."

"There aren't any virgins older than fifteen, except for women nobody has asked. Like Cassandra. Poor, peaked thing, no man could put up with all that wailing. If she had once stopped, she might have found a lover. Ajax only raped her because he caught her between wails, while she was praying to Athena."

"Nevertheless, you are not to touch Mellonia." His voice was quiet, but it was one of those rare times when he was father before he was friend.

"Very well, Father."

"Unless," Aeneas added thoughtfully, "she were your wife. Seventeen women on our ships, and the youngest well over thirty! If you are to wed at all, it must be a native of this land. And Mellonia stirred you, didn't she? I mean, with more than desire. I saw it in your eyes."

Ascanius said with surprise at his own intensity: "Why yes, she did. A man wouldn't tire of her in a night—or even a month."

"Or even a lifetime," said Aeneas softly.

"Father, why don't *you* wed her? I watched your eyes too."

"I've killed two women already by marrying them."

"What in Hades do you mean? The Hellenes killed my mother, and Dido killed herself!"

"Because of me."

"Oh, Father, sometimes that little boy in you is so stupid I want to spank him. Let's go home."

Aeneas knelt on the bank and, speaking slowly and gesturing with his hands, asked Delphus to follow them by way of the river. The dolphin answered with what sounded to Ascanius like the clicking of knucklebones over a tile floor.

"What did he say?" asked Ascanius, who had never bothered to learn the language of the dolphins.

"He says he'll beat us to the ships."

Arm in arm, bows over their shoulders, they started for the ships.

"Our men could use fresh meat," said Aeneas. "Our bread is moldy, our cheese isn't fit for a rat. Another cake of meal will turn my stomach. But where are the animals?"

"We've scared them away by talking."

"Utmost silence then!"

But not for long. In a laurel grove, behind the feathery, aromatic foliage and the yellow-green flowers, flanks glittered, hooves thudded among ferns. Ascanius fired an arrow even as Aeneas raised a restraining hand.

"Father, I've shot a deer! Why did you try to stop me?"

"I'm not sure it was a deer."

They parted the foliage and found their quarry lying among violets. He wore no garments, and his four legs and silken flanks, seen from a distance through leafy branches, might have been those of a stag. But his arms and chest were those of a youth, and his young face seemed made to smile. Ascanius and Aeneas crouched beside him. In the lionskin bag hanging from his neck, there was a comb of tortoiseshell and a tiny alabaster vial of sweet-smelling resinous liquid. He was dead, of course. Ascanius' aim was unerring; Aeneas had taught him, and his arrows were feathered with Harpy feathers. Already there was a buzzing around the body. Aeneas smote at the insect with his hand. A bee, not a fly, it vanished into the forest.

"Father, I have done a terrible thing. I thought—I thought—"

"I know, Phoenix. You've never seen a Centaur before. I should have been quicker to stop you. We are equally to blame. We have murdered instead of hunted."

CHAPTER III

As she walked toward her tree, bemused, absent-mindedly plucking a narcissus only to scatter its petals after her and ignore the impulse of pain from the broken stem, she thought: *I am seventeen. It is time for me to visit the Sacred Tree. It is time to bear a child. I will ask Volumna's permission.*

Most of her friends had already visited the Tree, but she had delayed until now; in fact, had ignored Volumna's reminder that the tribe was in need of girls to rear instead of boys to expose. ("Our numbers are dwindling. Why, one of these days we may be forced to take husbands, like our disreputable sisters to the north. May lightning strike me first!")

She had talked with some of her friends. No, they could not remember what had happened in the Tree. They had entered the oaken door and lain among downy leaves; slept and dreamed. What kind of dreams? Sometimes dark and disturbing. The evil dwarf-god Sylvanus came to them in nightmares too horrible to remember. Sometimes disturbing but decidedly not dark. A "golden pain" was the phrase Segeta had used to describe her first visitation from the god. "And when I knew myself with child, the pain was forgotten and the gold enveloped me like autumn leaves."

Still, Mellonia had delayed. She had enjoyed her friends; she had picked mushrooms with them in the forest; alone, she had gardened and woven and baked and read papyri from her chest. If she was not happy as she had been as a little girl, she did not demand happiness. Contentment with the task of the moment; wistful but not anguished rememberings of the time when her mother had shared her tree; adamant refusal to think about the future: it had been enough.

It was no longer enough. Her change in mood puzzled and disturbed her. Usually she liked mysteries. Were most men evil or merely crude and ignorant? Why had Rumina wed the god Ruminus and yet forbidden her mortal daughters to wed either human or Wanderwooder? She liked mysteries but not in herself. It angered her to feel unaccountable feelings, to perform uncharacteristic actions. She had just murdered a narcissus. Unlike roses, which shuddered if you so much as sniffed them, narcissus were not particularly sensitive flowers. Nevertheless, she had felt its tiny pain without remorse. Yesterday she would have left the flower on its stem. She had just decided to visit the Sacred Tree. Yesterday she had felt no urge to sleep and risk disturbing dreams and bear a child who might be a boy.

Perhaps the change had something to do with the strangers, Phoenix and Halcyon. Surely it had something to do with them. *It's because they're men,* she decided, *and I liked them, and now it won't be a horror to me if I bear a son. I will ask Volumna if I may rear him in my tree and hope that he will look and act like Halcyon. The Dryads to the north do not expose their sons. Why must I? I will speak to Volumna.*

She had liked both of the strangers. Phoenix had reminded her of Bounder, pretty enough to admire, earthly enough to tease. Yes, earthly, that was the word, and she was at ease with the things of earth. Like Bounder, he had stared at her intently and looked as if he wanted a kiss, but she had not been angry with him. (Males of all races seemed to set great store by kisses.)

As for his brother, Halcyon, he was not in the least like Bounder or Phoenix. The silver hair: snow in the boughs of a tree. But the tree was green. She had sensed a sadness in him much older than his young face, but there had sometimes been a child's twinkle about him too. She felt drawn to him in a way which she could not understand. She wanted—what? To

29

touch his hair. To touch his cheek with her lips. Like a daughter—except that he did not look old enough to be her father. Like a sister—except that he was a man and men were said to be brutes. But she had found him kind. Her feelings usually drenched her like a cold spring shower or warmed her like a hearthfire or burned her like hot coals from an overturned brazier, and she had no difficulty in knowing what she felt at what particular moment. Now, it was as if she were being drenched by a shower and warmed by a hearthfire at the same time. At least she was not being burned by the coals!

Suddenly the forest seemed hostile to her. She wished for her tree. Lions were rare; roguish Fauns were frequent but a nuisance, not a danger. Perhaps it was not a fear which hurried her steps but the aloneness of the place. Oak, myrtle, elm. Thicket of brambles, clearing of grass. She felt their emanations like little gusts of chilling wind. They did not dislike her but they did not companion her, not in this part of the forest. She wished for wisps of smoke from the hearths of the Centaurs, but their compound lay too far to the north. She wished for the singing of a Dryad as she combed her hair, but these oaks were not inhabited, nor did they invite inhabitants. She wished for her friends, Bounder or Bonus Eventus. She wished most of all for the Sacred Oak.

There, there, at last, a little apart from the other trees though still a part of the Dryad circle, surrounded by grass and daisies and a garden of lentils and lettuce, stood the oak which was her home. She called it "Nightingale" after the bird she loved the most, the plain brown little bird which opened its beak and sang more silverly than a lyre. The tree was as old as the forest, as large in circumference as a small hut. Her mother, her grandmother, how far back had her family lived in that tree? Since the time when Saturn had ruled in the land and women had married men instead of fought against them; before the coming of lions; before the coming of wars. She would live until it died, unless she was struck by lightning like her mother, or killed by a lion or a blood-sucking Strige—or, as Volumna liked to warn, a human male. If she died, the tree would continue to flourish so long as it was inhabited—and loved—by a member of her family; if the tree died, she herself would die.

She opened the wooden door, red with the dye of the cochineal, and entered the trunk. The tree was not hollow as strangers sometimes supposed, it was alive, and to live it must hold sufficient wood for the sap to flow from roots to branches. But it was so large that her first ancestress had carved a narrow shoot, like a well, all the way up the trunk to the branches, and cut rungs into the wooden walls. Large trees were tough; they did not feel such things, or if they felt they shuddered and then accepted, glad to make room for life, for children, as it were, to inhabit them (like a Dryad who had lain in the Sacred Oak?).

Inside the door, an olive oil lamp burned constantly in a niche and lit the way, step over step, to the hut which sat in the branches like a great beehive: a round hut of willow boughs bent to peak at the top and honeycombed with a dozen round windows which could be closed with parchment in the winter for the White Sleep but opened in spring to admit the daffodil-whispering breezes, the complaints of the grass as it clawed its way through the earth and finally thrust its blades to the sun. In the single room, which was fragrant with bergamot and mignonette and other such flowers as could be plucked without inflicting pain upon them, there was a couch of lionskin stretched across a wooden frame. A hand-loom. A box of hammered silver to hold the gems—topaz, porphyry, moss agate—which she found in dry stream beds or lodged among roots and traded with the Centaurs for grain and vegetables. Three tables hewn from a dead elm tree, with small bases and bulbous tops and resembling large mushrooms, one for meals, one for the varicolored yarns which she wove into tunics and cloaks, one to hold a daisy growing in an urn shaped like a water lily. And finally a chest with round slots for her beloved papyri. Hellene, Latin, Egyptian—the roaming Centaurs, those restless linguists, had brought these tongues and scrolls inscribed with them from the far edges of the world.

She had understood the brothers when they had

31

spoken Dardanian, one of the Hellene dialects, and Halcyon had said to Phoenix: "I hear something in the woods." (She had wanted to say, "You had better speak Assyrian if you don't want to be understood!") She herself was limited in her travels. In a single day from her tree she would pale and start to feel listless; in five days, she would pine and probably die. But she traveled through her scrolls. She knew about the fall of Troy from an eyewitness account by a Hellene scribe; she owned a copy of the Egyptian Book of the Dead; and her own people were famous for their dirges, collected into a scroll, about winter and the death of leaves and the sorrow of bearing a boy instead of a girl; and their paeans about awaking from the White Sleep and running barefoot over the new-grown grass to greet their friends.

But she did not feel like reading poems or histories or scrolls of any kind.

She lay on the couch and felt as if she were rolling in sun-warmed leaves and started to dream a waking dream. Rock crystal wind chimes tinkled sweetly among the branches around the house and wafted her spirit to the heart of the Sacred Tree, dim and enigmatic but no longer threatening. Someone was watching beyond the door. A Dryad? A man. Halcyon. His face was kind and sad and he moved toward the door. No, she wanted to cry. It is forbidden to men! Even to other Dryads when one is "couched for the God." *Yes,* she wanted to cry. *Risk the danger, come to me in the Tree, your eyes as blue as a halcyon feather, in place of a god whose face I have never seen!*

Ah, such sweet and impious dreams might come unbidden in the night but she did not have to endure them in the afternoon. She sprang to her feet and peered through one of the windows and breathed the leaf-cleansed air and felt the kindly emanations of her mother tree. Had it been a presentiment? Dryads were sometimes blessed or cursed with intimations of the future. Impossible! A vagrant fancy, and not to be indulged. She would fetch some cheese and wine from the basement lodged among the roots. She would bake some blueberry cakes for Bounder in the small brick oven and—

A bee spiraled in one of the windows.

"Bonus Eventus!" she cried, inexplicably glad to have a companion, however small. To Fauns and Centaurs, to any untrained eye, bees were either small or large—honeybee or bumblebee or mason bee—otherwise indistinguishable. Bonus Eventus was a honeybee but slim for a drone, almost as slim as a worker, and almost hairless, with wide transparent wings which were his special pride. There was always a scent of myrrh about him, and when he rested against her breast she felt a faint rumbling of contentment. Vain? Of course. He felt assured that the queen would accept *his* favors at her next nuptial flight. Indolent? Of course. He slept in flowers instead of gathering myrrh to manufacture honey. But he was also loyal, and she loved him as a true friend, as Halcyon loved his dolphin, Delphus, and she dreaded the fact that his little life, so lately begun this very spring, must end with the fall.

"You're just in time. I was going to fetch you some honey from the basement." Being a drone, he was sometimes denied his supper by the intolerant workers. "Do you think I'm pretty? Bounder said I was."

But she saw at once that he had not come to exchange compliments for honey. He was not wheeling happy arcs of pleasure or gratitude, but tracing a ragged pattern of pyramids.

"Come. Beware. Danger."

She pressed her hand to her hair and feeling among harmless ornaments—hawk moth of malachite and porphyry dragonfly—felt the lethal pin like a tiny sword. It was dipped in the venom of a large, hairy spider called the Jumper, with green eyes and sharp mandibles. It was deadlier than a Strige.

"Lions?"

A quick downward spiral. "No."

Then he spurted from the window. Whatever the danger, she was meant to follow him.

Bounder appeared to be sleeping in the sun. He had learned some indolent ways from Bonus Eventus, and he liked a nap in the afternoon. There was no sign of violence. The grass was not scented with lion or wolf, nor wet with blood. But when she knelt, she saw that his eyes were closed more tightly than with sleep, his lips were twisted with pain, and deep in his breast lodged the telltale arrow, feathered with Harpy feathers.

Which of the brothers had killed him, she did not know, but they seemed to her equal in guilt. Had they not hunted together? It mattered little which had raised his bow.

Bonus Eventus lit on her cheek as lightly as a tear.

Her mother had died in lightning and she had sat at her loom from sunrise to sunset, ten days in a row, singing the old lament, "Only Night Heals Again." Every year, before the assuagement of the White Sleep, she grieved for the falling leaves and the wilting flowers. But these were part of the natural order of things, the way of the earth, the forest, Rumina's divine plan. This was invasion, however, this was murder. Volumna had told her the truth about men, particularly Aeneas' men, it would seem. And what of Aeneas himself? Old, battle-scarred, no doubt, accumulating crimes as if they were acorns to string on a necklace.

Anger clawed at her throat like an ice-encrusted branch.

She kissed Bounder on the mouth. "It is my last gift except one," she said. "And it comes too late."

But there was still the last gift.

She had only to follow the Tiber to find the Trojan ships.

Five ships, cabinless except for canvas stretched across the decks as makeshift roofs: Their bronze-jawed dragon bows were moored to trunks, their oars had been lifted from the water and laid along the open areas of deck. Fifteen ocher moons had been painted on every hull to signify their long years of voyaging. The sails which had once been white, lowered now, were rent and soiled by many winds. It might have been a straggling pirate fleet instead of the remnant of the once formidable navy which had guarded the entrance to the Black Sea and the fields of grain which were called the Golden Fleece. It might have looked pathetic if she had not learned the identity of its sailors. Was Aeneas as

34

cruel as those two treacherous brothers who should have been known as Hawk and Falcon?

She knelt—and listened—and heard. She did not comb and pin her tresses above her ears out of vanity, but to sharpen her hearing against the approach of lion —or man. The Trojans had made a camp on the shore. They moved among tents of tattered sailcloth, a few women among them, poor bedraggled things in robes which hung like dead brown leaves to their ankles (where were the bell-shaped skirts the Trojan women were said to have borrowed from their Cretan ancestors?). The men, for the most part, were bearded and scarred and mature if not elderly. They wore loincloths of sheepskin, except for two men who patrolled the camp in battered armor, holding crooked spears and looking too tired to hurl them. There, too, was that trifling Faun, Mischief, who had brought the Dryads news of Aeneas' arrival. Now he was ingratiating himself with the Trojans, scratching his stomach, stomping his hoof, making them howl with laughter—and no doubt telling them news of the Dryads.

And there of course were the brothers, standing apart from the other men and talking to each other with great earnestness. She could only catch some of their words at such a distance. They had killed a Centaur. . . . They must return to find his body. . . .

Horror flapped in her like a bat. Doubtless they meant to lash his hooves to a pole and bring him back to their camp and roast him over a fire! They would feast and drink and dine on the flesh of the land, and tomorrow the tired spearsmen, one as bristly as a boar, one too young for a beard, would doubtless wake refreshed and invade the woods for another night's feast. She only wondered how Mischief had escaped the pot. Perhaps they hoped to keep him as a spy.

"Aeneas!" It was the beardless spearsman who spoke.

Her ears stiffened at the name.

Halcyon-Aeneas turned to face the man who had called him. "Yes, Euryalus."

"Will you need help?" Euryalus was about her own age, she judged. He must have been a baby when Troy fell. His cheeks were as pink as the inside of a triton

35

shell. It was the pretty, smooth faces which hid the greatest treachery, she decided.

She stepped out of the trees. "Aeneas," she called.

Halcyon-Aeneas looked at her with surprise and what she would have mistaken for pleasure if she had not learned the wickedness of his heart.

"Mellonia. You've come to visit our camp. I hoped you would. You left before I could ask where you lived."

"I thought your name was Halcyon."

"I told you it was," Ascanius-Phoenix hurried to say. "We're new to your land. I didn't want my father recognized until we knew who you were. He has many enemies."

"Now you know me. I commend your piety. Where are you going?" Her heart beat like a moth in a spider's web; lies were hard for her. But she had a good teacher.

She held her ground as Aeneas walked toward her. She could outrun him and he did not hold a bow. She could easily dodge a spear from one of the guards.

"Mellonia, my son and I have made a terrible blunder. We mistook a Centaur for a deer, and—"

"I killed him," said Ascanius. "It was I who made the blunder, not my father."

"My son had never seen a Centaur. Neither had I since I was a small boy. I should have stopped him, though. Now we are going to bury him."

Bury him? Skin him was nearer the truth! "I'll take you to him," she said. "You may lose your way in the forest. Just the two of you, though. It would not be respectful for more to come."

"But his friends," said Ascanius. "Won't they be angry and try to harm us?" He turned to his father. "I think we should take Nisus and Euryalus with us."

"I will explain to the other Centaurs what happened. They are a kindly race. They will understand, if you give him the proper rites."

Aeneas and Ascanius walked toward her.

The coolness of their cunning! Why, they had even fixed their features into expressions of pain. Aeneas at least. Ascanius looked more concerned for their safety than sorry for Bounder. But Aeneas might have been grieving for a lost friend. With just such a look he had no doubt confronted Dido before he deserted her.

They will try to take me, she thought. *Perhaps they will try to kill me. But the sea and the ships are their strength. The forest is strange to them.*

It has fallen to me to kill Aeneas.

CHAPTER IV

Mellonia tried to walk ahead of them, but Ascanius, shovel over his shoulder, kept abreast of her and looked from time to time at the pale, rigid features so recently as fresh and piquant as a lotus blossom. He had liked the forest when he and his father had swum in the Tiber with Delphus, and talked of cities burned and cities to build, and watched Mellonia materialize from the trees, a girl with green hair and pointed ears and a curiosity to rival that of Pandora. He had thought: At least my father has found a country in which to build his second Troy, fulfill his destiny, and satisfy the gods—to rest and grow young with me. Perhaps he has also found a wife to help him forget that long-faced Dido. Even Orestes finally escaped from the Furies.

Still, there had been a doubt. Mellonia was more than a girl; she lived in an oak tree and spoke of mysteries and hid as much as she said. Had not Pandora released a box of misfortunes into the world?

Now he was more than doubtful, he was frightened, and fear was rare in Ascanius; not caution, but downright bone-chilling fear. He was not particularly remorseful at having killed a Centaur. He rather imagined that Centaurs, being half horse, were limited in both intelligence and feeling. He had killed men deliberately in battle, many of them. Why should he grieve at having killed a horse-man which he had mistaken for a deer? But he felt his father's pain with an almost physical intensity. That was Ascanius' blessing, that was his curse, to love Aeneas more than any other man, woman, or god. As for himself, he was a warrior, neither more nor less; he liked to fight; he was not a killer but he was not squeamish when he had to kill; he even liked this wandering life and rather thought that he was meant to be a pirate instead of inhabit and behave in a city. Certainly he had never regretted the cities which he had put to the torch. As it was, however, those implacable ladies, the Fates, had woven his destiny into the same design with that of Aeneas. Cut a single thread and both men suffered the same misfortune. They might have been Castor and Pollux, brother and brother, instead of father and son. If his father asked him, he would even have built one of those preposterous Egyptian pyramids (with the help of a few thousand slaves).

One thing he refused to do: Allow Aeneas to be endangered by a disconcerting girl who lived in a tree but who, in spite of her virginal airs, probably rolled in the grass with any Centaur who gave her a whinny. He had been too young to protect his father from Dido, that devious queen with eyes of burning pitch and the cry of a tropical bird surprised by a lion. Aeneas' gentle but firm authority had led the Trojan exiles through even more dangerous trials than Odysseus had faced, but his defenses against a helpless or helpless-seeming woman, alas, were not those of Odysseus; they were about as adequate as acorns hurled against Amazons. But Ascanius was five years worldlier now than in what he liked to call "Dido's den." He knew about women: What they were good for (except for his mother, little more than to tease the eye and warm the bed); and when to beware of them (most of the time, and especially when they cried or smiled or avoided looking at you).

The silence of the forest began to grow intolerable. Ascanius was almost indifferent to flowers. Vaguely he noted an abundance of daisies in the open spaces, but could not have named those tall purple flowers on spiky stems which grew among them. But he instantly noticed sounds, footprints, signs of danger. There were no sounds now except their own feet padding the grass, Mellonia barefoot, he and his father sandaled with Egyptian antelope leather, and that in itself was an ominous sign. As long as they followed the Tiber, with Mellonia on the forest side of them, he felt relatively safe, but when they left the river and plunged among oak trees as hoary with moss as a sunken ship with barnacles, his muscles tautened, his vision intensified, and he watched Mellonia like a cormorant watching a fish, but with the suspicion at times that she was the cormorant, he and his father fish (here in the forest, perhaps, he should change his simile to eagle and hare).

"Father," he said. "Do you realize we're two miles from the ships? I think we should let Mellonia and her friends bury the Centaur." Her upswept hair was tumbling over her ears; she had torn her tunic in several provocative places (one breast was almost exposed). All in all, so it seemed to him, she had very calculatingly become a Dryad in distress.

"It isn't far," said Mellonia quickly. "Just beyond that copse of elms."

"How do the Centaurs bury their dead?" Aeneas asked. His voice was grave and hushed; there was such a tenderness in his eyes that Ascanius wanted to shake the wretched girl for exploiting his father's sympathies.

"In the earth, where else?"

(And shake her too for her impertinence.)

"I mean, do they raise a funeral pyre and burn the body first?"

"No. They dig a space and cushion it with grass. And stretch the body as if it were asleep, and include a few possessions which might be useful on the journey to the Underworld."

"What prayers do they pray?"

"They make up a prayer for the occasion. They are natural poets and words come easily to them."

Bounder's body had not been moved or disturbed. Except for the pain in his face, he still had the disconcerting look of one who had fallen asleep in the sun. Aeneas knelt beside him and smoothed the lines of pain around his eyes and mouth.

"He was just a boy. What was his name, Mellonia?"

"Bounder."

"How did you happen to find his body?"

"Bonus Eventus led me here."

"Did Bounder believe in Elysium?"

40

"I don't know that word. He talked about a meadow and an oak grove where there was never a White Sleep, and Dryads lived in marriage with Centaurs. He once said he would like to marry me. I thought he was teasing."

"Don't your people ever marry Centaurs? They seem a noble race." (Noble! Well, there was a certain nobility about the horses which drew a great warrior's chariot—Achilles' steed Xanthus, for example. But who wanted to marry them?)

"Never."

"I'm sorry. I think he must have loved you."

"He kissed me once. I'm not sure what he meant. It seemed to please him."

"Did you love him?"

"Love him? He made me want to run in the grass and swim in the river. He made me think of beginnings. I went with him once to see his newborn brother. He was trying his spindly legs, and I was happy when he learned to stand. I fed him honey cakes and I wanted a child of my own. Even a little boy with horns. That's all I know. Sometimes I was angry with him, but never for long."

"If you don't marry the Centaurs, who fathers your children? I have never heard of a male Dryad."

"We go to our Sacred Tree and wait for our god Ruminus. But please—I don't want to talk about such things now." She led them across the meadow to a space of sand and tiny stones.

"Here is the place to dig his grave. There are flowers around it but the spot itself is bare. A thunderbolt landed here. You won't kill anything except a little grass."

Mellonia stood apart from them, watching their efforts with a mixture of expectation and perplexity. Had she expected them to skin the Centaur and make a rug from his coat? Ascanius in turn watched her, covertly but with the wariness of one who had never lived in a time of peace or sailed on a sea without the threat of a storm. The bee-tipped pin glinted in her disheveled hair. He watched her hands.

They lined the grave with sweet-smelling grasses and settled the body among them with tender hands.

41

"Strew him with violets. They are pretty flowers but with little feeling. They don't feel pain when you break their necks. He liked them. And leave the bag around his neck. He was never without his comb and scent bottle."

Aeneas drew the ring from his finger, a black pearl which had come to him from his father, and to his father from Aphrodite. It was very dear to him, large as a small coal, a dark smoky gray which smoldered in the sun.

"To pay Charon," he said. "In Troy we used to place a coin under the tongue of the dead man before we laid his body on the funeral pyre."

"It is a beautiful ring," said Mellonia. "I wish—I wish Bounder could have worn such a ring while alive. He was very proud of the way he dressed. I used to tease him. 'You're vain,' I said. 'Yes,' he answered. 'To please you.'"

"May I say a prayer now?"

"Yes."

"Persephone, you have known what it is to be stolen out of the sun and into the dark. You were just about Bounder's age, I should think, when Hades carried you into the Underworld. You loved violets too. Hyacinths and columbine. Companion Bounder in his first loneliness. Show him that asphodels too are flowers. Weave him a garland to wear around his neck."

Mellonia not so much interrupted as continued the prayer, though she substituted the Latin name for the deity:

"Proserpina, comb his hair for him, will you? His arms aren't long enough to reach the end of his mane. Good-bye, Bounder. Dream of me while you sleep and I will bring you violets and kiss you on the lips."

"If you dream of Phoenix and me," said Aeneas, "may it be as men who mistakenly did you a terrible wrong but would have liked to be your friends." Then he whispered a poem which, like much of his poetry, pleased but puzzled Ascanius:

"Purple is distance;
    Hyacinth over the hill,
    Tyrian murex.

Purple is distance only:
Violets wilt in the hand."

He turned from the grave and silently, motionlessly started to cry. As a little boy, Ascanius had seen his father cry when Creusa was lost among the ruins of Troy; again when they left Carthage and Aeneas saw the smoke of Dido's funeral pyre, and again after a battle in which a friend had been killed.

Ascanius threw his arms around him as if he were comforting a little child. "Hush, hush, my dear. You mustn't cry for my foolishness."

Aeneas returned his embrace; you forgot how strong he was until you felt his powerful arms. Where other men smelled of leather or bronze, Aeneas smelled of the sea—its foam and its salt-fresh winds. Even his silver hair, pressed against Ascanius' cheek, was crisp with salt. Ascanius knew that he was not weeping for the death of one Centaur; his griefs had accumulated like frost on the deck of a ship, and he wept for the world's lost youth; for the golden city stricken by another gold called fire; for those who had loved him and gone to join Persephone. At such times, you could only hold and warm him against the frost of memory.

Just for that little moment Ascanius forgot to watch Mellonia. When he remembered to watch her, she had drawn the pin from her hair and she stood as still as the tree in which she claimed to live. She might have been grown from the earth instead of born to a Dryad mother. Even her arms, raised in front of her, seemed frozen in the air like delicate branches.

He stepped behind her, encircled her with his own, anything but delicate arms, and pressed her wrist cruelly until she dropped the pin. Anger scraped in him like crusted barnacles. He wanted to break her neck.

"Which one of us were you going to stab?"

"Aeneas first. Then you, if I had the chance."

She did not ask for mercy, nor did she seem to be angry or frightened. He could have crushed her in his arms. How small she was! Such tiny bones—and the faint rapid heartbeat—how did it sustain even so small a being? Her hair seemed spun out of leaves and sun-

43

beams. And yet she had meant to murder both of them.

"But you didn't," said Aeneas. "Why didn't you, Lady of the Bees?"

"At first I thought you had killed Bounder for game, for food. But then you dug a grave and picked violets, and your eyes were windows into your soul, and I saw a pain which made me yearn for you."

"And my son?"

"He loves you. Thus he is part of you. I couldn't hurt him."

"Let her go, Phoenix."

Reluctantly Ascanius released her and quickly retrieved the deadly pin. "I wouldn't have hesitated to kill *you*," he said, "if I had known you planned to hurt my father."

She smiled at him. "But that too would have been a kind of love, wouldn't it? I can't be angry with you, Phoenix. We're much the same, after all. We are willing to kill for those we love."

"Shall we be friends, Mellonia?" Aeneas asked. It was one of those invitations which no one ever refused. Inwardly, Ascanius sighed. The only time he envied his father was when Aeneas made a conquest with a smile, and then refused what he had won, while he, Ascanius, in spite of his looks—and he was not unacquainted with mirrors—must woo with gifts and compliments.

She took Aeneas' hand and pressed it to her cheek. There was no coquetry in the movement. It was as simple and artless as Ascanius embracing his father.

"What a small hand you have for a great warrior. Younger, even, than your face. A boy's hand," she said. "Bounder wouldn't want you to be sad for him anymore. Neither do I."

She dropped his hand and shook her head violently. A curl quivered above her ear like a tendril of grapevine. "I can't be your friend even though I want to."

"What do you mean?"

"My people have taken an oath to kill you. You shouldn't be here now. Return to your ships and never come here again without your men. Never swim in the Tiber without Delphus. And beware of oak trees. The ones which look as if they were listening."

44

Aeneas gripped her shoulder. "Mellonia, you're not going to run away again?"

"I must."

"But how can we see you again?"

"I must speak to Volumna, but I think——"

"What, Mellonia?"

"That she will not change her mind. That she will tell me I am a foolish girl and it is time I visited the Tree."

"To be got with child?"

"Yes. Volumna says that a baby cures her mother of childish fancies. If it's a boy, she hardens her spirit as a tree its trunk. If it's a girl, she learns self-sacrifice, like a bush giving its branches to the birds."

"But I don't understand about this tree. You say a god will come to you there?"

"He will come in a dream, and then I will bear a child."

"But gods don't come in a dream if they mean to father a child. Or goddesses either, if they want to be mothers. When Aphrodite came to my father, she was very real. He never tired of telling about her. Hair the color of lapis lazuli. A gown which shimmered as if a spider had woven it. And—well, such specific details, and so many, that he couldn't have dreamed them all." (His father was being discreet, Ascanius reflected; those "specific details" had included a manual for lovemaking which only the goddess of love, or a highly skilled courtesan, could have mastered and taught.) "Why, she even gave him the ring I placed on Bounder's finger."

"Our god is different. You might say he whispers a child into our wombs. Please let me go now. The danger is very real to both of you. The Dryad trees—the listening oaks—are some distance away, but Volumna often comes to this meadow to pick the violets."

He released her instantly. "Then come to the ships again——"

Already there were oak leaves closing behind her, almost as if she had opened and shut a door.

Aeneas moved to follow her. Ascanius seized him roughly by the arm—his own father, the son of a goddess!—and stepped in front of him.

"Father, no! Didn't you listen to her? You'll get

45

yourself killed and her too, and I'll have to chop down every tree in this Zeus-forsaken forest to get that bitch she calls a queen!"

There was fire in Aeneas' eyes. Calm, deliberative Aeneas, aroused to wrath! *A blow of his fist will break my jaw,* Ascanius thought. *But at least I will stop him from chasing Mellonia. He will have to carry me to the camp and then he will feel too ashamed to leave my side until he is sure I will heal.*

"There's another way," Ascanius pleaded, though quite prepared for a broken jaw. "We'll find out about the Tree from Mischief. And about Volumna. Then, whatever you decide I'll follow you."

Ascanius felt his father relax between his grip. "You would have hit me, Phoenix, wouldn't you? To keep me out of danger."

"Tried, at least. And slung you over my shoulder like a deer and carried you back to the camp. That is, if I had gotten the first blow, which is very unlikely. Otherwise, you would have done the carrying. If there was anything left to carry."

"I think," said Aeneas, "that this is the first time in my life I'm grateful that someone wanted to knock me unconscious. No, the second. Remember the time Achilles almost killed me? Overturned my chariot and tried to run me down?"

"I was not yet five. But yes, I remember. How could I forget? The whole city was watching from the walls, including Mother and me."

"The very next morning, I meant to face him again, in a battered chariot drawn by weary horses. That night your mother kissed me and served me wine. 'A rare vintage,' she said. 'And rarer in Troy after so long a siege. It will help you to sleep.' It was heavily drugged. I slept for three days. During that time, Achilles caught an arrow in his heel."

"It seems I inherited Mother's selfishness. I don't want to lose you."

Back at their camp, they found Mischief amusing the men with a dance and a song so piercingly sweet that one thought a nightingale must be imprisoned in his flute. The dance was a curious mingling of leaps and whirls, and he danced with a grace belied by his cloven

46

hooves and his shaggy frame. He stirred one's blood; one's feet seemed to move of their own accord; one's loins yearned for the woman he had never met, the Nereid under the wave, the goddess in her cloud:

> Queens walk in the dusk.
> Listen!
> Their antelope sandals hush the grass.
> Shall Helen, mute,
> Forget the tumbling jonquils of her hair,
> Ungarlanded?
> Queens walk in the dusk. . . .

Aeneas too felt the magic. Music was wine to him and he often led the men in the Dance of the Crane, learned from the old Cretans.

"Mischief," he called at last, shaking himself to break the spell. "Will you come to my tent?"

Mischief flung the flute to Euryalus and shambled after Aeneas and Ascanius. His head lolled to the side; the fur on his goat-like flanks was matted with cockle-burrs; he wore a perpetual grin not unmixed with guile. Music had made him a demigod; now he was a clown. Ascanius, however, did not think him as stupid as he tried to look.

"Mischief," Aeneas asked, "there are no female Fauns in Italia, are there?"

Mischief drooped his head. He smelled of sweat and rancid fish. (The Fauns fished eels from the Tiber with nets of animal hide.)

"No, my king."

No one else called Aeneas "King," though except for the Trojan War he would have sat on a gypsum throne and ruled Dardania. He did not like the title. He remembered the one who should have been his queen.

"But you must need women. In my part of the world, your people, whom we call Satyrs, have always been known for their womanizing. Or are you like the Achaeans—Achilles and Patroclus—and satisfied with each other?"

"Only when women are scarce."

"And when they aren't, where do you find them?"

"The Volscian women rule their husbands in their

homes. But in the woods, they like a bit of sport, and we rule them." It was hard to imagine any woman succumbing to Mischief. Perhaps at times he exhaled an irresistible musk, concluded Ascanius. That, and his music, and his overgenerous endowment, an enviable characteristic of his race, and the fact that most women want to be bedded as badly as men want to bed them, perhaps explained his boast.

"Who else? The Volscians live at some distance, I believe. King Latinus and his people still further."

"The Dryads! They're the best. Sweet as a honey comb!"

"But Mellonia told us they never take husbands or lovers."

"We take *them*."

"You ravish them?"

"You might call it that. While they're sleeping in that hollow tree of theirs. It's midway between this camp and the circle of Dryad oaks. You follow the Tiber till you come to a lightning-blasted stump. Then, a javelin throw from the river, is the Tree. It's dead, of course. Gnarled and crooked. Like a big gray viper standing on its tail."

"They must sleep very soundly."

A huge grin split his face. His teeth were surprisingly clean and small.

"They do. There's enough for three or four of us to visit the same Dryad. You see, they drug themselves on the juices of the poppy."

"But don't the other Dryads try to stop you?"

"There aren't any close enough. It's one of their customs. The Dryad who wants a child comes alone to the tree. In she goes and bolts the door behind her with a big oak timber. But a long time ago, we dug a tunnel right up through the roots and into the chamber where she sleeps. It's dark in the Tree. Even if she woke, she wouldn't see us coming. Or leaving, as happened a time or two to me. I was overzealous and aroused her from sleep."

"And then they bear your children and thank Ruminus."

"Who whispers into their wombs," muttered Ascanius.

"Yes, and they must like it, even in their sleep. They keep coming back. Dryads live as long as their trees, you know. Often they bear as many as twenty children. If the child is a girl, she's kept, since the girls resemble their mothers. Pointed ears but that's all. If the child is a boy—tail, hooves, hairy flanks—they expose him because he looks like us, though of course they don't know why. They have some silly legend that a long time ago one of them lay with a Faun and put a curse on the race, and the curse repeats itself in every boy. They leave him under a tree for the lions to eat. We rescue some of them, though, and raise them to be our sons."

"And no one even suspects?"

"I don't know. Volumna isn't a fool. But if she knows, she keeps it to herself. My father had her. And my grandfather. They said she wasn't bad. Maybe she's waiting for me."

"Do you know the Dryad named Mellonia?"

"How could I not? We call her the Lady of the Bees. Still a virgin, poor thing, and afraid to visit the Tree. But Volumna is going to make her go before long. I overheard her talking to the girl's aunt, Segeta. Have I told you what you want to know?"

"Yes."

"Give me a dagger."

"Your hooves are weapons enough."

"A loincloth then?"

"With all that hair? You're born in a loincloth."

"The female Centaurs make fun of my nakedness. They won't let me in their compound."

"Very well."

"And a flute? Mine is wooden. Euryalus has one of tortoiseshell. I like his better."

"I'll speak to Euryalus."

"And rings of gold for my horns."

"We have none. We are very poor."

Mischief shrugged. "Supper then. Something different from roots and berries and woodpecker eggs."

"Ask the men to feed you. Nisus over there will give you some cakes of meal. And, Mischief . . . one thing more."

"Yes, King Aeneas?"

49

"If you touch Mellonia"—his tone would have chilled Achilles—"you or your friends, I will kill you and use your pelt to make a rug for my tent!"

Mischief lost his smile. There was no awkwardness in his departure. He left behind him a few hoof prints and an odor of fish.

"I think," smiled Aeneas, "that we should burn some laurel branches in our tent." Then, seriously, "We must warn Mellonia. I don't trust Mischief. Or his friends."

"How will we find her?"

"We already know how to find the Tree. And Mischief will doubtless know when she plans to 'await the God.' He seems to know everything. Did you ever notice the size of his ears? I'll go there alone and guard her myself."

"You won't go anywhere alone. Her people may sight us along the way. In these parts, it seems, even the bees tell tales. I'll go with you and stand watch at the mouth of the tunnel."

"If I ask you to stay in the camp?"

"No."

"If I order you?"

"No."

"To avoid getting knocked down and slung over your shoulder like a deer, I suppose I will have to agree."

"That's sensible of you, Father. But is it so horrible that a Faun should take Mellonia? They aren't all like Mischief, I should hope. And she seems to want a child. If it weren't for the Fauns, her race would die."

"No man is going to take her, Faun or otherwise! Not against her will."

"Father, you haven't looked this way since you met Dido. You're such a trial to me with your women. You mistake them for goddesses and then forget that even the Olympians have their failings. Grandmother hasn't exactly been a faithful wife, has she? I mean, she's married to Hephaestus, but that didn't keep her away from Ares or Zeus or Grandfather. I wonder if I'll ever rear you into a safe old age."

"Don't worry, Phoenix. I don't mean to take her for myself. Not even in marriage."

"Why not? I don't particularly welcome the prospect

50

of a Dryad as a stepmother—this one is much too pretty. But you would do her a singular honor."

"I'm more than twice her age."

"How many times have people mistaken you for my brother instead of my father? One of these days, I'm going to look like *your* father. Besides, you're a long way from that last ferry ride over the Styx."

"Yes, but is Mellonia? I mean, if she marries me?"

CHAPTER V

The Dryad oaks formed a rough semicircle among larger groves of beech and elm. A stranger might walk among them and mistake the sweet hum of their looms for industrious insects; mistake their doors for cracks in the bark. The little beehive houses sat secretly among the branches, invisible from the ground except for an occasional glint of brown which seemed a part of the tree.

Only a stranger would walk into this circle, or a Centaur, or Mischief or another Faun who, in spite of his bestiality, might be useful; or a Volscian maiden; and the stranger, if he were male and human, would hear a hum not of looms and feel himself prickled with tiny darts which seemed no more painful than bee stings, but killed in a space of seconds with the poison of the Jumper; or perhaps assaulted by actual bees and stung to death, though the bees too died in the act of stinging and the Dryads only used them against a terrible threat.

It seemed to Mellonia that Volumna had never looked more serene and confident as she stepped from her tree. It was hard to believe that she did not live in one of those storied Cretan palaces, now in ruins, where queens had sat on griffin-flanked thrones and bathed in marble tubs with silver spouts. The upswept swirling silver of her hair, still faintly touched with green, might have been leaves mantled with frost. The body beneath the green tunic was sapling-slender and fragrant with many myrrhs. She had ruled her people for almost three hundred years, and made them feared and respected in the Wanderwood. She had fulfilled her self-appointed destiny. She walked in the tranquility of her power and achievement.

Aeneas and Volumna, though enemies, had much in common. Both were leaders. Both were ripe with years, even to the silver of their hair, and yet they were somehow young. But there was a difference as great as that between the sea and the forest. Aeneas was not tranquil. Aeneas was still tormented by self-doubts, and in his anguish, it seemed to Mellonia, lay his grandeur. No leader had earned tranquility while those around him suffered pain. Bounder had died; Aeneas, not Volumna, had grieved for him, and not only because his son had shot the fatal arrow. ("All things die," Volumna had said to her. "And after all, he was only a Centaur—and male at that.")

"My daughter, I am pleased that you have chosen to visit the Tree. You have robed yourself as becomes your mother's child. The God will be pleased." Mellonia's customary garment was a simple tunic and perhaps a pair of sandals; but now she had dressed herself for receiving the God: anklets of malachite, that smoky green jewel which looked as if it had come from a deep forest whose shadows were touched but not effaced by sunlight; armbands of emerald and chrysoprase; a fillet of silver inlaid with porphyry nightingales to bind her hair; a halcyon wrought of chalcedony and suspended from a chain around her throat.

Yes, thought Mellonia, *but you would not be pleased if you knew that I would rather have a boy than a girl; that I am not going to let you expose him; and that I would visit Aeneas at the ships and tell him of my plans if I were not afraid of being followed and caught and increasing the danger to him. What is more, I am going to name my boy "Halcyon."*

("Were you in love with Bounder?") ("I don't know. ... He made me think of beginnings.") *Am I in love with Aeneas? I don't know. He makes me think of beginnings—and forever. I want to touch his hair and kiss his cheek, and yes, I want to kiss his mouth. Strange that the touch of mouths—even the thought of touching—can stir me in such a fashion. I feel as if*

53

friendly bees were creeping over my skin. I am like the hyacinth. When the dragonfly descends from his celestial garden, she shudders with the peril of his assault (I have heard her shriek). And yet, at last she bathes him joyfully in her nectars and seeks to withhold him from returning to the sky (I have heard her weep).

"Come, we will go to the Sacred Oak. Levana, Segeta!" Her voice rang like a conch shell through the trees. Doors opened. Two Dryads advanced to meet them. Others watched them from their huts among the branches. Volumna was quiet but luminous. Her tiny sandals left hardly an imprint in the grass; almost, she seemed to float like a morning mist. *(She is anticipating a girl, an increase in the tribe,* Mellonia thought.)

Levana and Segeta, both of whom had borne a number of daughters, began to discuss the joys of motherhood.

"My first was a son." Segeta shuddered. Her hair was the dusky green of moss and her words were hushed and hoarse as if they came from a chamber among the roots of a tree. She had borne seven daughters and three sons and her age was reckoned to be above two hundred.

"A hideous child. Horns, hooves, hair, and little else. It was not hard for me to expose him. But when my first daughter came, I sacrificed a honeycomb to Rumina."

"But the Tree," Mellonia asked. "What did you dream in the Tree?"

"I've told you a dozen times that I don't remember."

"Not once?"

"Not once. A shape seemed to move in the darkness. I was afraid. The first time, at least, there came a stabbing of pain in my womb. But when I awoke and wandered out into the light, I felt a great peace. And in less than a month I knew that I was with child by the God."

"And you, Levana?"

"The first time it was not Ruminus who visited me. It was the evil dwarf-god Sylvanus. He tortured me in my sleep. I awoke with bruises in a pool of blood."

"What was he like in your dream?"

"He had horns, but crueler than those of a Faun. Gnarled and mossy like ancient branches. And he was

54

gross, gross, in his male parts, and to look upon him filled me with disgust."

"Hush, Segeta. He rarely comes anymore, and only to those who have lost the God's favor. I recall that before your first visit to the Tree, you were overfriendly to a Volscian boy."

"We played knucklebones by the Tiber, that was all."

"That was enough. Mellonia, I trust, has in no way angered the God. Have you, my dear? As for the Tree, I can only tell you that it is a mystery. How the God performs his miracle, who shall say, except Rumina? Speaking for myself, I seemed to see his face, smooth as the tender bark of a sapling, and I felt neither fear nor pain. As you know, I have visited the Tree more than twenty times and given eleven girls to the tribe."

(*And exposed ten boys. Why did you tell me that men—all men—are evil—and that Aeneas must die?*)

"Go now, Mellonia. We must leave you at the edge of the meadow. And when you awake, you will not need to ask about mysteries. Your mother was my dearest friend. Your daughter shall be like my own granddaughter." (*And my son?*) "We have need of valorous women to guard these woods against barbarians like Aeneas."

"Perhaps," said Mellonia, "he will sail away with all of his ships."

"Perhaps. But turn your thoughts to the God. Leave the demons to me."

A flask of burnished amber hung from a chain around her neck. She removed the cork.

"Empty the flask, Mellonia."

The liquid was dark and sweet—rather like grape juice thickened with honey, but acrid with the soporific juices of the poppy. The three Dryads watched her as she crossed the last space of meadow to the Tree. She wanted to call to them, "Wait," when they turned and disappeared into the wall of forest. But even as she entered the Tree, turning the wooden door on its ancient leathern hinges, she felt a drowsiness stealing through her limbs, like the lethargy of one who has fallen in the snow. She burrowed into the soft dry leaves and stared at the tenuous rim of light which outlined the door. She could not discern what objects shared the Tree with her. She closed her eyes when they began to burn and gave herself to the company of leaves and the pleasant, barky scent of the air, and perhaps a woodmouse, sharing the same warm nest, and, finally, the spirit of the God. She felt him like a hearthfire. She knew why her friends talked of being cradled by his warmth. It was as if he were enfolding her in his arms, and for the first time she could envision his face. Ruminus. Father. God. Meaningless words, in the past, to her whose tribe painted no pictures and carved no sculptures. But now she imagined his face and his body too, and she was not surprised that he resembled Aeneas, the son of a god; the godliest of men.

Do I wake or sleep? Surely no sleep can bring so sweet a dream. . . .

I sleep and await the coming of the God.

But now the fear . . . a faraway sound like the crisp dry crackle of leaves, but growing, heaving, shuddering under this very Tree. Cries. Blows. A trembling of the earth. The God and Sylvanus have met to war for me.

("Sylvanus has horns, but crueler than those of a Faun. . . .")

She was not alone in the room. Someone had come to her from the earth's dark catacomb. She felt the heat of his body, she heard him breathe, and then, in her dream, he materialized above her, lucid in the dark, and every feature belonged to the God, to Aeneas. Joy opened its petals in her breast. *The God has won. I will bear a son, I will bear a son. . . .*

In her dream, she called to him: "Ruminus, bring me a boy-child with your own features, Aeneas' features. I will nurture him to manhood and make him the lord of the forest!"

He knelt; she felt the touch of his warmth; her body yearned to his hands; but his hands eluded her.

A chill seemed to grow between them. *It is not enough. He has visited me but not yet breathed his spirit into my womb. He has found me unworthy of his love. I will bear no child, neither boy nor girl. This is the greatest terror. Not the assault of Sylvanus but rejection by the God.*

"Please, please," she cried. "How have I offended you?" The cry had broken her sleep. Awake and waiting, she lay in the warm leaves, but she knew such a coldness as no fire but one could warm.

A figure moved between her and the rim of light in the door. She could not distinguish his shape, nor even hear him breathe until he approached her. Ruminus or Sylvanus?

"Who are you?" Again, with sudden anger. "Who are you? Have you rejected me?"

Silence enveloped her like a falling of leaves. "Sylvanus?"

She reached for the pin in her hair. Did evil gods feel pain?

"Mellonia."

The voice held the deepness of the pounding surf and the sweetness of a seabird calling to his mate across the hushed waters of a halcyon sea.

"Halcyon," she cried. "For a moment I took you for Sylvanus." She reached out to him and took his hand and drew him beside her and pressed her head against his shoulder. His arms enclosed her as gently as sunwarmed moss, but he was redolent of the sea; he smelled of salt and foam, he did not need to speak of journeyings as far as the Isles of the Blessed and battles where men were heroes instead of demons. *High on the windy plains of Troy.* . . . The loss of the God seemed little compared to Aeneas' coming. But the child—the child. . . .

"Halcyon, the god visited me, I think, but he did not leave me with child. I know . . . already I know. He left me with an ache of emptiness."

"Mellonia, there is no God. Not one who comes to you in this Tree. The Gods live on Olympus or under the earth or in the sea, and sometimes they come to us—truly—and we are blessed or cursed, as they choose. But Ruminus, I think, never comes to your people. Not here, at least."

"But if not the God—Halcyon, what are you saying? Someone fathers our children. Or does Rumina alone breathe life into our wombs?"

"No, Mellonia."

"Then who—?"

57

"The Fauns."

The truth gnawed at her entrails like one of those slimy crabs at the edge of the sea. The Dryads to the north, the Faun-lovers, the despised and fallen: Was it the same with her own people? Of course it was the same. Why had she failed to guess? Her fear of the Tree had reflected a secret doubt.

"Like Mischief."

"Yes."

"And one of them tried to come to me while I slept. And you protected me. That was the sound I heard in my sleep."

"It was three of them. But Ascanius helped me to break a few horns. He's guarding the entrance until we leave."

"They would have taken me in my sleep, one after the other. Like animals."

"Yes. Like animals. But animals can love too. When I was a little boy, I watched a she-wolf die of grief after hunters killed her mate. The Fauns would have taken you with lust, not love. But Bounder—wasn't he half an animal? And yet he loved you. Would it have been so terrible if he had made love to you?"

"When he kissed me, I was angry and afraid, but only at first. Later, I wanted you to kiss me."

"I wanted more than a kiss. The touch of lips is an act of love, but lips are only a little part of a loving body. Even in the Underworld, our souls are clothed in bodies, and souls cannot touch without their garments. When I wed Creusa, I was not yet twenty and she was just fifteen. We were both virgins. I had been much sheltered except in the arts of war. I had never known the caresses of a friend or a girl. We were clumsy and frightened, and all the time our relatives were laughing and shouting jests outside the bridal chamber. But I made love to her in my awkward fashion, and shame left us, and we were one with each other in every way. Ascanius was born to us of that union. Can such a boy spring from an evil act?"

"I know how he loves you," she said softly, "and how both of you miss Creusa. He is a fine son to you."

"And you think Creusa and I were loveless animals?"

58

"No, Halcyon."

"And Dido. I loved her with a dark hunger. With little sweetness and much pain. But not with evil."

"She was honored by your love. You offered her life and she chose death. She was a shameful woman."

"An unhappy woman who mistook summer for spring and wanted to stop the drip of the water clock, the shadows on the sundial. I must leave you now, Mellonia. Wait a little before you go from the Tree, and then you may tell your friends that you have forgotten what it was you dreamed. You won't be the first not to bear a child after a visit from the God."

"But I shall never come here again and be taken in the dark by someone like Mischief."

"Then give yourself in the light to someone who takes your heart before he asks for your body. There will be other Bounders."

"He was a brother to me. I know that now."

"There will be men not brothers. Perhaps—my son?"

"No!"

"Mellonia, you do him an injustice. He is very fond of you."

"Oh, I like him well enough. It's just that I would always be thinking of someone else."

Aeneas gave a little sigh of perplexity. She could not see him in the dark but she could imagine his smooth brow contracted with doubt. He was, after all, a child with women. Her seventeen years weighed heavily upon her. In the time which it takes for a morning glory to open her petals, she had learned the truth about the Tree and the truth about her own heart, and yet it was Aeneas, not she, who was lost for words. Wise Aeneas, who knew men's hearts and led them through years and perils, was as ignorant as a Faun of a girl's heart.

"Foolish, foolish Halcyon. It's you I love!"

"Ah," he said, all anguish in that cry. "Creusa loved me. Dido loved me. They are ashes now. To the women I love I am death. Perhaps it is a curse put upon me by Aphrodite because my father revealed their tryst in the forest."

"I think you left your curse in Carthage, or else it fell into the sea during a storm. At any rate, you've lost it somewhere, and I don't feel in the least threatened with being reduced to ashes. It's true my mother was struck by lightning, but she was ninety-seven years old, and I am seventeen."

"I have to build a city. You have to live in a tree."

"Build it at the mouth of the Tiber—with a high wall, of course, to keep out lions—and I will come to you whenever I can."

"And risk Volumna's anger?"

"Sylvanus take Volumna! It might do her good. Halcyon, are you refusing me? If you are, I won't be angry. You never asked me to love you. I have lived in the Wanderwood for all of my life. What have I to offer to the hero of Troy, the fabulous voyager, except that I can weave you a tapestry or a tunic. Repair the sails on your ships. Paint their hulls. I can play the flute better than Mischief and sing as sweetly as the nightingale and much more cheerfully. I can even read scrolls, Egyptian and Hellene, to say nothing of our own Latin. Did you know that, Aeneas? And I ought to be quick to learn a wife's most important skill." (He was looking perplexed; she could tell from his sigh.) "I refer of course to the couch. All of those little tricks which make a man prefer it to any other piece of furniture." (She had read of such things in her scrolls but hurried over the passages; she would have to return to them with a studious eye.) "I'm a poor little thing, I suppose, after the queens you've known. Creusa, who mothered your son. Dido with eyes like burning pitch. But Bounder said I was pretty. Am I pretty, Halcyon?"

"Pretty is a word for daisies. You are a hyacinth, miracled out of the earth by the slender hands of Persephone."

"I'm very fond of daisies. They are much more lovely and sensitive than you suppose. But I know you intend a compliment. Will you kiss me, Halcyon? I want to start practicing. Otherwise, we may bump noses."

"If I kiss you, I will forget my years and my curse. I will make love to you like an animal and like a man. You saw Ascanius and me when we swam in the Tiber. You said you were not frightened by our naked bodies. Was that the truth?"

60

"I thought you beautiful, just as I said. I liked the difference of you. Even that appendage you males so like to vaunt."

"In Dardania, we had a saying which my father taught me. He said he learned it from Aphrodite. 'Love is a dragonfly.' Do you know what that means, Mellonia?"

Why did the dear, maddening man continue to spout his pretty speeches when lips were better used for kisses? Well, she would match him image for image until he wearied of poetry and remembered that poems do not create love, but love creates poems.

"That it comes swiftly and by surprise."

"And may leave as swiftly."

"Everything leaves," she said. "But it comes back again. When I lie down for the White Sleep, I am fairly certain that I will wake with the first stirring of buds. When I lie down for the last sleep, I expect to awake in that place you called Elysium and find my mother and Bounder waiting for me. And you. Shall I tell you what you are to me?" And then she sang:

> "Bird of the moon,
> Halcyon
> Risen from the mica seas
> Beyond the ebony abyss of night,
> Descend,
> Descend
> And silver me, dark earthling,
> With your lunar foam."

"It isn't my own, of course. My mother taught it to me, but I did change 'sea gull' to 'halcyon.' But I think we have had enough of poetry, my dearest Halcyon. Shall we pretend that we are going for a swim in the Tiber?" She raised her tunic above her head and flung it onto the leaves. Pins and anklets and armbands followed necklace until there was nothing left to remove except the porphyry fillet in her hair, which she threw across the room as one might discard a withered garland.

"Are you ready for a swim now, Halcyon?"

"Yes," he whispered.

She tossed open the door so suddenly that it fell from its leather hinges and sun streamed into the Tree and kindled Aeneas' nakedness into a wonder of bronze.

"Mellonia, someone may see us!"

"My people could learn a great deal from watching us. So could the Fauns."

"But my son—"

"How does he think he got here? Surely *he* doesn't still believe in Sacred Trees."

The hyacinth, wearied by her long climb from earth's brown citadel, her struggle to open her petals, sleeps in the dew, dreams in the sun. To sleep and dream ... to sleep and dream. Is it not enough?

But listen! The whir of wings. . . .

CHAPTER VI

Ascanius sat beside the ant-marauded tree-stump which, together with wild grapevines, concealed the tunnel entrance to the Sacred Tree. He sat and waited and envied, a little, his father in the Tree. What a perfect chance to play the Faun!

"I'm just going to make sure that she's all right," Aeneas had said. "A dark tree can be a frightening place, when you wait for a god, and the god has other plans."

"But, Father, this is the best prospect Mellonia will ever have to be properly got with child. Why not father a prince while you have the chance?"

"Phoenix, that would be rape!" His indignation could not conceal his temptation. Ascanius knew him like a clay tablet. In spite of his continence, he was no less tempted than other men; more, when he fell in love.

"Call it what you like, you'd be doing the girl a favor. When she wakes up still a virgin, I promise you she's going to be disappointed."

"When she wakes, I'll tell her the truth."

"Why not let *me* tell her?" Ascanius grinned.

"Because I don't trust your methods."

"Such a waste," Ascanius muttered, nursing a bruised jaw and (watchful for ants, telltale bees, or devious Dryads) settling among the vines so recently tangled by their bout with three muscular Fauns who had used their horns as both clubs and knives. "Such a sinful waste. Grandmother would not approve. . . ."

But here was his father, staggering out of the tunnel as if he were climbing from the Underworld or, to judge from his face, descending from Olympus. So Anchises must have looked after his tryst with Aphrodite. He looked twenty instead of his usual twenty-five and his eyes were so blue that one thought he must have stolen their color from his mother's sea-twinkled hair.

"Father, you don't have to say a word. You told her all the way."

Aeneas sank beside him and only Ascanius' arm kept him from lurching into the trunk. He blinked his eyes and smiled and seemed to be looking into his own mind and enjoying what he saw.

"She liked me." (His voice was a sigh.) "Phoenix, she liked me."

"I heard you the first time, in spite of the mumble. Loved you, I would say."

"Well, possibly. She *said* she did. She woke from a nightmare and threw her arms around me, and what could I do but try to comfort her and tell her about the God? We talked for a long time and—and—she wanted to bear my child."

"And you act surprised. I knew as much when we met her at the Tiber. It wasn't *my* child she wanted, or the God's either. I shall just have to get used to the thought of a little brother or sister with green hair. I'll be quite jealous at first, you know. I'm sure you'll spoil him terribly."

"Have I spoiled you?"

"Terribly."

"She may not have a child. I'm a bit out of practice. Five years since Dido—"

"You don't forget that sort of thing. It's like shooting an arrow. By the way, how was she? Being a virgin and all that. She *was* a virgin, wasn't she?"

"Of course she was!"

"Well, she was a very old virgin at seventeen. She must have been oversheltered by her mother. What I was about to ask was, did she please you? Sometimes they squeal and twitch at the wrong moment and all you can think is: At least I've made it easier for the next man."

64

"Phoenix, Ruminus should strike you dumb for saying such things!"

Ascanius was unperturbed. He knew when his father was truly angry with him, about once every five years. He knew now that his father wanted desperately to talk about Mellonia, but that his sense of propriety restrained him from the more intimate details.

"Well, he hasn't, any more than he came to Mellonia. Come on now, Father, we'd better head for the ships and maybe you won't be so secretive on the way. After all that waiting, I want to hear *something* about your conquest. Among hungry men—and may I remind you that I haven't had a woman in three months? —a feast should be shared, at least with one's devoted and famished son."

"This was a wedding feast," said Aeneas quietly. "You're right about one thing, though. It won't do to be seen by the Dryads. They may come back to see Mellonia home to her tree."

"Will she be safe? You can be quite sure that the Fauns we manhandled will tell Mischief, and Mischief will tell that Gorgon, Volumna."

"I intend to send word to Volumna that I consider Mellonia my bride and that if any harm comes to her, she can expect an ax in her trunk."

"You have just told her, Aeneas, Butcher of Troy, betrayer of women. I will repeat your son's question. How does it feel to despoil a virgin?"

Volumna stood athwart their path as immovable as a tree, and much more threatening, and looked at least twice her diminutive height. Ascanius had never met the formidable woman, but he recognized her from Mellonia's description. She made no move to reach for the lethal pin she wore like a bee in her hair. There was sufficient menace in her stance and stare.

"As you guessed, I returned to see why Mellonia had lingered in the Tree. I have found my answer."

Aeneas was no longer the dreaming and slightly befuddled lover. He was first of all a king, and no mere rusticated queen was going to intimidate him, even in her own forest.

"I have taken a bride, and not against her will," he said with an evenness belied by his blue eyes, which

65

had turned gray with anger like the Aegean at a blast from Triton's horn. "I will visit her whenever I choose, and she will come to me at my ships, and if you harm her—well, you have overheard my threat. It is not an idle one. I would burn a city to protect Mellonia. I have burned them before for lesser reasons."

"To fell a few trees is a little thing for Trojans," added Ascanius. He did not like the woman; in fact, he disliked her more intensely than any other woman since Dido. "We may be wanderers, but we keep our axes sharp. Battle-axes. Some of the timbers in our ships have started to rot. How would you like your oak to repair our hulls? Or we might make some new oars from your branches."

There was something alarmingly spider-like about her. She looked as if she could spit poison like the Jumper. Perhaps it was the way her green eyes stared at one without ever blinking, and her cheeks began to bulge, as if she were gauging distances and gathering venom in her mouth.

"Only if it dragged you into the haunts of the octopus and the shark. You know we will die without our trees."

"Not right away," said Ascanius. "Not until we've had some sport with you and your people. Fifty women-starved Trojan males. Think of that, Volumna. Raunchy rutting males who will settle for anything between twelve and five hundred and then swap with their friends. Our own women are a bit weatherbeaten from the sea. But you Dryads keep your looks to the end, don't you? Even you, Volumna, and you must be all of three hundred. I rather fancy you for myself. I've always liked older women. They know more tricks."

"Come, Phoenix. We've told her our intentions. Mellonia is safe, I think."

"One more thing, Father." Then, to Volumna: "You knew about the Tree all along, didn't you?"

She stared at him with stupefaction. Momentarily he was almost sorry for her.

"About the tunnel. And the Fauns," he persisted.

"I don't know what you mean. The God comes—"

"Yes, in the shape of a shaggy Faun."

"What sacrilege is this? Why, the God should snare

66

you in one of his branches and strangle you with your own hair."

"Don't play the virgin with me, Volumna. Mischief told me about the Tree. He's been there many times himself, and both his father and grandfather have been there with you. You may be pleased to hear that they found you adequate even in your sleep. If you *were* asleep."

Volumna looked like a frostbitten tree. Three centuries weighed like snow upon her shoulders. She looked even less than her height of four feet. She swayed and seemed about to fall. Aeneas tried to steady her but she wrenched away from him. (*She is the only woman,* Ascanius reflected, *who has ever refused my father's arms; if possible, she is more stupid than a Cyclops!*)

"I will tell you a story," she said in a voice like wind rustling among parched leaves.

"A true one?" Ascanius asked.

"Alas, yes."

"Father, I don't trust her. I think she's trying to keep us here till her friends arrive."

"I swear by the nurturing breast of Rumina that I came alone, and that no one followed me."

"Tell us your story," Aeneas said.

"In the early time my people wandered happily and fearlessly through these woods and mingled with the Fauns. The Golden Age had fled from the land with Saturn, and the Silver Age had fallen upon us as imperceptibly as an evening mist. But silver is also good. The Fauns were much less bestial then. Idlers as always, but mirthful and, when they chose, gentle. They were the only males in these parts—the Centaurs had not returned from their pilgrimage to the East—and we tolerated them as lovers if not as husbands. I was a small child at the time. I did not know of such things as lust and procreation, and lightning was the only danger I knew.

"That was before the coming of the lions. There had always been wolves and bears, but we had lived in harmony with them. Never hunted them. We had no darts, no poisons. We trapped small game in nets and grew vegetables in our gardens and slept the White Sleep when the food was scarce.

"One night we had met in the circle between our trees for the Festival of Rumina and Ruminus. It was spring, and the air was awash with the scent of clover and bergamot. We were dancing the Dance of the Spring Awakening, and the cry of flutes muffled all other sounds. Suddenly they were among us, lordly creatures with tawny skin and noble manes. We had never seen their like. Had they sprung from the moon to join our festival? Climbed from Proserpina's kingdom? We would have shared our feast with them. Our wines and our cheeses.

"But they had come for another feast. My mother and I were close to our tree. One of them knocked her to the ground. She was very strong, and she was afraid for me. She used her flute like a dagger and drove it into his throat. He roared with pain and writhed away from her, and together we fled behind our oaken door. The other Dryads were less—or more—fortunate. None of them escaped. Even my mother had hurt her back in her fall. She lived only a year. Together we visited the Fauns and traded gems for food. (With their palisades and their slings, they had learned to withstand the lions.) She taught me how to weave and read a scroll and smell a lion at a hundred yards, and then she died and left me, still a girl, to the long loneliness of being the only Dryad, and the only female, in the Wanderwood. I wanted to die. I thought of killing my tree. But the Fauns seemed to pity me. They continued to bring me food. I had a friend named Shag-Coat. He was about three—that is to say, eighteen of your or my years. Fauns do not age as you and I, but as the goats they resemble. He showed me what my mother had not known, how to extract the poison from the Jumper and arm myself with darts or pins.

"'Shag-Coat, you're such a good friend,' I said. 'How can I pay you back? I can weave you a tunic, except that you never wear one. Or make you silver tips to protect your horns.'

"He laughed. 'It's too soon, little one. Wait.'

"Another year passed. I was thirteen. 'You can repay me now,' he said. 'Meet me in the Sacred Oak of the god you call Ruminus—the one we know as Faunus. Shut the door after you to keep out lions.'

68

"I waited in the leaves and darkness. He came to me through the tunnel.

"'Shag-Coat,' I cried. 'I've been so afraid without you. I thought of lions and Jumpers and wanted to open the door and run into the sun!'

"'You needn't be afraid anymore,' he said. He laughed and took me among the leaves. He was very strong, and he smelled of musk which made me light in the head. I fought until my hands were bruised and raw. It was no use. He took me without a kiss.

"'Now you have repaid me,' he said. 'And in a little while you will see the gift I have left you.'

"In a little while I was with child. I bore him a daughter. I thought: I will destroy her. But the Goddess spoke to me in a dream. 'And destroy your race? Your daughter must bear a child. Despise the Fauns but use them to your own purpose, as they have used you.' In the end, I myself took her to the Tree and gave her a poppy drink to cloud her senses. 'The God will come to you,' I lied. I did not want her to know the truth. Can you understand that, Aeneas, the Butcher? No one has ever learned the truth among my people."

"It would be better," said Aeneas, "if they knew and chose."

"What is there to choose among Fauns? They are much the same. Animals who walk like men."

Gently he touched her shoulder. "There is love as well as lust. Some of my men want wives."

"I would sooner bed with a Faun."

Ascanius sat with his father and the Trojans. Nisus and Euryalus, the bearded and the beardless, leaned against each other in the firelight and did not appear to notice the yearning faces of women who, thirty-five, looked sixty, because they remembered a wooden horse and columns like dragons of fire, a king who was stabbed and a queen who was dragged into slavery. The older men could have passed for pirates—as brown and cracked as old sailcloth—except that for fifteen years they had followed Aeneas and taken a special light into their eyes.

Mischief was whirling around the fire, his cloven hooves as nimble as the feet of a dancing girl, his nightingale flute piping a crystal song. He stopped, suddenly, in front of Aeneas.

"My king."

"Yes, Mischief?"

"Sing for us, will you? There is a song in your breast. It is wrong to keep it caged."

Ascanius was quick to echo Mischief's plea. He too had seen the song; he wanted somehow to join in the music from which he had been excluded since the afternoon.

"Yes, Father. You haven't sung since we came to this land. I restrung your lyre, you know."

Aeneas smiled and shook his head. "It is a private song."

"Is it about love?" Euryalus asked.

"Yes."

Euryalus and Nisus looked at each other and spoke in a single voice: "Sing it for us then."

Aeneas sprang to his feet and seized the lyre from Ascanius' outstretched hands. He began to play, plucking the strings so lightly that they hardly seemed to move. It was as if he were releasing their music instead of imposing music upon them. Then he sang, and his people watched him with such an adoration as only gods command, and truly believed him, it seemed, the son of Aphrodite, but would have adored him no less had he been the son of a kitchen maid. Ascanius loved him with adoration too, but also with the sweet familiarity of one who knew him as friend before father, and father before god; with such a love as Satyr-may-care young men do not often know and scarcely understand.

"The Lady of the Bees

"Carnelian, emerald, and chrysoprase,
    Topaz, lemon or green,
    Moss agate, and the smoky malachite,
    Serpentine:
    These were the gems she wore;
    And birds of porphyry
    To bind her hair, and warm against her throat
    Chalcedony.

70

Acanthus, lavender, and mignonette,
Hyacinth, purple or blue,
Narcissus, and the feathery tamarisk:
These she grew;
Clover and columbine
And wilder bergamot
To scent the hall, and for its bee-frail buds,
Forget-me-not."

No one spoke. What were mortals to say when a god had sung? Battle-bruised warriors wept openly beside the piled canvases of their sails. A ghost of beauty flickered in the sea-wracked faces of women who had known another hall and other flowers.

But Aeneas was not sad. He had sung a praise and not a dirge. He had sung of today and not yesterday. Quietly he smiled, no longer needing to remember. . . .

As if the song had conjured her out of the trees, Mellonia stepped into the circle of the fire.

Aeneas went to her and drew her among his friends. She came without shyness and listened when he spoke to them:

"You have followed me for fifteen years, and some of your friends have died for me, and perilous times are still ahead of us. But as you are my friends, befriend Mellonia too, my beloved and my bride."

The men rose and stood in their places, and Mellonia walked among them, trailing the scent of bark and bergamot behind her, and even Mischief's face seemed transfigured into a brief nobility. It was Euryalus, the lover, who said:

"Lady of the Bees, loved by the man we love second only to each other, Nisus and I commend our lives to you."

An old woman as wrinkled as sun-baked bricks—she had been a handmaiden to Queen Hecuba—said: "Troy has found a second queen."

"I think," said Mellonia, "that the sweetest thing in all this forest, in all that world of your wanderings and beyond, is that a man and a woman, or a friend and a friend, should know each other, with their bodies as well as their spirits, and rise like a single flame on the hearth of the Goddess." Then, to Aeneas, "May we talk, beloved?"

71

Ascanius tried to leave them—he was, after all, a separate flame—but she called after him: "You must come too, Phoenix."

They walked to the edge of the Tiber where it broadened to meet the sea. Delphus was circling slowly in the water, watchful for sharks or Carthaginian galleys.

"There are no sharks here, Delphus," Mellonia said. At the sound of her voice, he paused in his circlings and began his fitful sleep.

"I am cold," Ascanius said, though the night was warm and the fires had been built to frighten lions and to bake fish in clay ovens. "I must fetch a cloak."

But Aeneas extended an arm to each of them and drew them beside him onto the grass.

"Ascanius and I will build our city a little inland from here. As close to your tree, Mellonia, as these ships. Whenever you leave your oak, may you come to me. Volumna won't dare to stop you."

Mellonia stared at the moon-dusted surface of the Tiber and Delphus, sleeping his eternally watchful sleep.

"Will she, Mellonia?"

"No, Halcyon."

Ascanius rose. "The moon is company enough for you."

"Please," she said. "Stay with us, Phoenix."

He could see the urgency in her face. If that Harpy, Volumna, had dared to threaten his father—

"Phoenix, I didn't like you at first."

He felt relief like a cool hand on his cheek. It was, he supposed, the need to confess which had troubled her.

"I know, Mellonia. We are very different, you and I. I'm not like my father. He's a god. I'm a pirate."

"We are more alike than you guess," she said. "It's true that you frightened me at first, but that isn't why I didn't like you. I was jealous, that's why! Because your father loved you so much that he seemed to leave no room for me. You see, Phoenix, I loved him from the first moment he turned his face to me in the Tiber." She spoke about him as if he were still in Carthage or Troy, and not beside her, looking more startled and pleased with every word. "Oh, he didn't see me yet. I

72

was well hidden among the trees. But I loved the youngness of him. And the oldness of him. And the joy of him. And the sorrow of him. And I was jealous. But now I love you as his son and also as my friend. Is it all right that I was jealous, Phoenix, just at first? I've felt such a tumult of feelings in such a short time! Like a flower who feels rain and wind and snow and sun in the same day. Hawkmoth and bumblebee and dragon-fly."

"It's all right, Mellonia. I didn't like you much either, and I suspect for the same reason, though I told myself it was because I didn't trust you."

"But that's in the past," Aeneas cried. "The night is for now." He sprang to his feet and pulled them from the ground and into his arms and whirled them in a great arc to the piping of Mischief's flute until they were laughing and gasping at the same time, and then they leaned upon him for support, and the column of his strength seemed able to resist all threat of ax or fire.

"I love you, I love you, I love you," he laughed. "My son and my bride. And no one—not Harpy or warrior or Dryad queen—shall ever divide us."

"You forgot time," said Mellonia.

"I defy time!"

"And yet it is time for me to go."

He looked at her with a puzzled urgency. "Go?"

She gave a wisp of a laugh. Deceit was hard for her. She did not fool Ascanius. If she fooled his father, it was only because she had first intoxicated him with her coming.

"Just for the night, my dearest."

"I had thought that you would stay the night with me."

"I am weary for my tree. Tomorrow, when I have rested, drunk her sustenance—"

"There are lions in the forest. Phoenix and I will see you home."

"No, I'm safer alone. I smell like an oak tree. You smell like fresh meat. But Phoenix will see me just to the edge of the woods. I have a secret to tell him."

"One you must keep from me?"

"Yes. Because I love you."

She took Ascanius' hand and drew him, half reluc-

73

tant, after her. "I'll soon send him back to you." He
saw the uncertainty on his father's face, but also the
inextinguishable joy. A boy's face in the light of that
orange moon, touched with the doubts, the sadnesses of
maturity, but boyish still in its unending capacity to
hope: Night heals, sun brings renewal and expectation.

"I'm not coming back," she said to Ascanius when
they were beyond Aeneas' hearing, shut from the camp
by slender elm trees which looked like Dryads dancing
in the moon. "I can't come back. Volumna has threatened to burn my tree."

Ascanius gasped. "To kill you?"

"Yes. She came with some of her friends and called
me down from my house—'Bring your hand-loom,
Mellonia'—and made me watch as they laid brush
wood against the trunk. 'I have only to strike a flint-
stone and the whole tree will become a pillar of fire.' "

"Can you find another tree?".

"No. The tree in which I was born will die with me,
or I will die with her. But Volumna has made me a
promise."

"What, Mellonia?"

"Not to strike the flint if I make a promise to *her*. To
leave Aeneas. Never to see him again."

"Of course you shall see him again," he cried, feeling
for his dagger, feeling warrior and son. "We've only to
capture the grove and save your tree. We can even
make you the queen!"

"Some of your men would die. We have our poisons,
you know. And stealth. And all of my people would die
before they would yield their trees. Yes, you could
probably capture the grove. The Fauns would no doubt
help you. They have never liked us, except asleep. But
I would live among corpses. Do you think I would
want to lose my people, Phoenix? I could leave them,
and gladly, if my blood were red like yours. But condemn them to death, never."

"They deserve no better."

"You don't know them. Some are my friends. Dearer
than Bounder, and just as innocent. Do you want to
kill them too?"

Yes, he wanted to kill them! It seemed to him that

74

there were two kinds of Dryad, Mellonia and Volumna, and Mellonia's so-called friends were like their queen, or why did they let her rule? But that, he knew, was one of his flaws; he was over-quick to anger and judge; unwilling to sift the amber from the seaweed.

"Do you, Phoenix?"

"No," he faltered.

"Tell your father that—that—oh, Phoenix, he does like pretty words, and I can't seem to think of anything. Except I'm glad he came to this land, and came to me in the Sacred Oak. He spoke of a curse. He thought he was going to hurt me. Well, he did. But I don't mind. Did you ever see those fat, silken lilies the Centaurs grow in their gardens? And tend and water and cover with moss in a heavy thunderstorm? They're pretty enough, graceful as hyacinths, but you won't find a true feeling among them. Cut down a flower, and what does the one beside her think? 'I'm glad it wasn't me.'

"I hurt your father too. But he was festering with old wounds. Perhaps in time he will see me not as another wound but as a salve of basil and hoarhound, which burns at first but finally draws out the pain."

She threw her arms around him and kissed him on the cheek, and they held each other in the chaste communion of loving the same man, and loving each other less for themselves than for the sake of him whom they loved in common, though except for Aeneas they might have been lovers.

"It's so much nicer to kiss a man than a woman. Especially my stepson. Go to your father now. Don't let him grieve for me. Take him in your arms as if he were a little child. You know how he likes to be held. Tell him it will make *me* sad to think of him sad. I'm not one of those pampered silken lilies. Not anymore. And whatever you do, don't let him follow me. Volumna let me come here. She will be waiting for him."

He felt a sweet burgeoning of love for her, a wolfsbane of bitterness at the thought of what she must lose. His father had his dream of a second Troy; she had—what?

"Where is Bonus Eventus?"

"Asleep in some flower, I expect. He'll wake me in the morning."

"But you said he would die in the fall. Won't you be lonely without him and Bounder—and my father?"

"And you, Phoenix. But the White Sleep will assuage me a little. Besides, I have learned how to wait. Go to your father now. And *keep him in his camp.*"

"I'll lie to him tonight. Then, tomorrow, I will drug his wine. Then if necessary I will sit on his chest with a club until I have made him understand!"

She called after him. "I'm going to bear his son."

"But it's much too soon to know."

"The Goddess told me."

For once he believed in her goddess. Perhaps Rumina was another name for Aphrodite.

"Phoenix."

He paused at the edge of the grove. "Yes, Lady of the Bees?"

"I'm going to live for a long time. When you're an old, old man and your father is dead, I'll still be much as you see me now. That city he's going to build—it may not be the one. The Second Troy, I mean, predestined by the gods. But in time there will be such a city, and somehow I think I'm going to be there to see it built. Who knows, I may help to consecrate the ground or lay the first stone! Anyway, I'll be keeping a watchful eye on your great-great-great grandchildren, and I can tell you now that they need never fear the forest, neither lions nor vengeful queens."

And then, the last puzzling thing she called to him: "I've thought of something to tell your father after all."

"What is it, Mellonia?"

"Love is a dragonfly."

Part Two

CHAPTER I

"He won't hurt you," laughed his mother. She did not often laugh, and the sound was as pleasant to Cuckoo's ears as the tinkling of wind chimes. But even her laughter did not reassure him. Seated on a three-legged stool in her many-windowed room, she was milking the mandibles of a Jumper, one of those huge, hairy spiders which supplied the poison for the weapons of the Dryads—the pins they wore in their hair, the darts they carried in pouches under their sashes.

His Aunt Segeta, sitting beside his mother, smiled her aloof, distant smile, and sounded as if she were speaking from the house in the next tree. Cuckoo liked her, but she never quite seemed to be in the same room with him. The souls of sleepers were said to leave their bodies at night and wander the wastelands of Nightmare or the Elysiums of Dream, and Cuckoo often wondered if only a part of Segeta's soul came back to her in the morning, and the other part stayed in a happier region, where Dryads had husbands and children had fathers.

"Cuckoo is more man than Dryad," Segeta said. "That's why he dislikes Jumpers." She was one of the few Dryads who spoke the word "man" without a shudder.

"And that creature knows it," said Cuckoo. "He would like nothing better than to bite the man part of me." By nature, Jumpers were peaceable even if poisonous creatures, but in an earlier time the Dryads had trained them to bite men and protect women, and their capacity to leap upon a moving target—that is to say, a man—was exceeded only by the swiftness and virulence of their poison.

"A boy ought to resemble his father,"said Mellonia. "But there's so much I can't teach him." She had never told him the name of his father; only that he was a Trojan, a warrior, a bard, and one whose greatness approached godliness.

"Even when the father was a Trojan? It's remarks like that, my dear, which keep you a virtual exile in your own tribe. Volumna might have forgiven you if you had ever admitted your error. You know how she loves to receive confessions. But you positively seem to exult in that unfortunate dalliance. She even resents my coming to call on you, my own niece."

"I want to go out," said Cuckoo suddenly.

"I'm through with the Jumper," his mother said. "I have enough poison to fell a lion. Segeta will take him back to his friends." The Jumpers lived in a cavern under Volumna's tree. ("They move about more at night," she often said. "Their rustling helps me to sleep. Sometimes I let them stay in the room with me.")

Mellonia lifted the Jumper onto the floor and Segeta whistled some low, thin notes. He walked crookedly across the reed-strewn room—his green eyes seemed to be fixed on Cuckoo—and Segeta scooped him into her hand.

"It isn't the Jumper," said Cuckoo. "It's just that—I want to go out." He could not tell her that it saddened his eleven-year-old heart unspeakably to see her in "virtual exile." Volumna did not keep her shut in her tree, but when she walked in the forest, no one walked with her unless it was Segeta or Cuckoo, and when she attended a meeting in the council chamber, she sat on the highest circle, with no one next to her, and he sat similarly islanded among the children, the one boy among thirty girls. It was not that the tribe disliked Mellonia. A whispered greeting, a smile, a gift of pomegranates—these things hinted that the friends of her girlhood had neither forgotten nor condemned her. But Volumna was fond of saying that anyone who befriended a "man-lover" was likely to follow her example and end by losing her honor and her reputation. Volumna's wrath, even her disapproval, discouraged open friendship with Mellonia. A Dryad queen could not execute her subjects, whatever their sins, even loving a man, but she could shut them permanently, eternally in their trees. She sometimes boasted that she had shown excessive leniency to Mellonia for the sake of her dead mother, "my dear friend."

"All right then, Cuckoo. I'll work on your new tunic. Segeta brought me some undressed yarn from the compound of the Centaurs."

He kissed her cheek and she held him briefly, tightly, and then let him go with a push toward the door. She always smelled of bergamot.

"Bring me some elderberries," she called after him.

"I can think of something better," he said.

"What?"

"My father."

"Amazon!" shouted the Faun, lowering his head to charge and butt, but changing his mind and scampering into a copse of elm trees when a stone from Cuckoo's sling racketed off his horns.

Cuckoo, four feet tall, stood his ground like a Centaur until the hoofbeats of his heckler mingled indistinguishably with the thrush-song and leaf-sound of the forest, the low continual music which only hushed with the night or the approach of a lion. When he was a small child, the Fauns had called him "girl" because he was smooth and neat. Now that he was tall, and still smooth of cheek and limb instead of hairy like themselves, they had found what they thought was an even less flattering epithet, since Fauns and Amazons sometimes made love but never liked each other. (His real name was "Halcyon," known only to his mother. "It was your father's secret name. He was a great warrior—the greatest. But the Dryads hated him. It is best not to speak it unless we are alone.") The others called him "Cuckoo" because they said that he was ugly like the bird, and because the cuckoo lays its eggs in the nest of another bird, and this Cuckoo had obviously been born into the wrong nest.

He gave a little sigh and lowered the sling. Some of the stones tumbled from the pouch attached to the sash of his tunic. He did not bother to retrieve them. Behind him, shut from view by the elms, the circle of Dryad oaks whispered with hand-looms and sang with the weavers' songs. He heard his mother, the sweetest among the singers, and resumed his mission with a forced enthusiasm.

"The forest is your friend," she had often said, but he did not feel befriended by these oaks and elms and laurels. Not that he was afraid. When one has been bullied by Fauns and ignored by Dryads for eleven years, there is little left to fear. But the trees did not companion him as they did his mother. They were simply trees, some handsome, some gnarled and hideous, and none of them spoke to him, nor did the flowers or grass. It was the animals he loved: the grizzled old bear who sometimes tried to steal honey from the Dryad hives and was pelted with stones by the angry owners (but Cuckoo took honey to his cave in a cup he had woven from lily pads); the dolphin, Delphus, equally old and scarred from a Triton's trident, who sometimes swam up the Tiber; even a toothless lion who lived in that part of the forest known as Saturn's woods.

A Dryad girl emerged from a copse of elm trees. She moved so languidly that she might have been sprouting instead of stepping from the slender trunks and the mottled green and white leaves. Her name was Pomona, after the goddess of fruit, and she reminded Cuckoo of a fig tree laden with figs, she was so ripe and succulent. She was Volumna's youngest child. At the age of twelve, to the consternation of her mother, she had already planned a visit to the Sacred Oak. But she was a tree with wasps. She always spoke the truth even if it hurt, and sometimes because it hurt, and she had a way of seeing more spiders than dragonflies.

"I saw the whole thing," she said, "and I was very proud of you." Cuckoo prepared himself for the insult which invariably followed one of her compliments. "Those shameless Fauns. Why don't they stay in their squalid little huts and not soil the rest of the forest? I can still smell fish in the air."

Perhaps, having insulted the Fauns, she was going to be agreeable to him. "Maybe I do look like an

82

Amazon," said Cuckoo, "but Bumper isn't going to say it."

"It's not so much that you look like an Amazon, though of course you do, being so tall. It's just that you're so ugly. Still, Bumper shouldn't remind you."

"No. Sometimes I forget and look into a stream, and there I am, half this, half that, not much of anything really. Hair neither green like my mother's nor brown like a Faun's."

"Yellow," shuddered Pomona, "and streaked with silver. Nobody has such a color. And do you have to wear that silly amulet? I never saw such a bird."

"It's a halcyon. A seabird." His mother had given it to him.

"A *sea*bird? I might have known. Your father came from the sea. A pirate, I believe."

"But I do have pointed ears."

"Yes, but the points are almost rounded. And your hearing isn't nearly as sharp as ours. Besides that, you're so big and clumsy. When you wear a tunic, you still look naked because it shows your legs, and most of you is legs. You're a good two hand lengths taller than me, and I'm exactly the right height for my age. Mother says so."

"I can talk to the bees. Better than you can."

"But you can't hear the flowers. You could step on a daisy and not even hear her cry."

It was true. He had often stepped on daisies as negligently as if they were insensitive narcissus, until a Dryad had reminded him of the difference by piling a handful of little mangled bodies at the door to his mother's trunk. "I expect one day you'll be too big for your mother's house. Then you'll have to leave the tribe."

"But without my tree—"

"Your father was a pirate, wasn't he? You ought to be able to live on a ship. Perhaps wood under you would be the same as wood over you, even if it doesn't come from your own tree."

Perhaps it was true. Perhaps he could live without his tree. But the time he had run away to the coast to look for a pirate ship, he had almost died.

83

"At any rate," she added, "you'll be no loss to the tribe."

"Oh, Sylvanus take you," he snapped and stalked into the woods. He did not know the meaning of the oath, only that it was vulgar, since he had learned it from the Fauns, and that the word "take" meant something more than "capture." Pomona, however, was unperturbed. She fashioned a nest of moss and, quite oblivious that she was crushing daisies, lay in the sun and called after him with a sweet but piercing voice:

"Jonquils are yellow. Pollen is yellow. But *hair*. Really, it's unnatural. Like a Triton without a tail. I expect Sylvanus was your father instead of that pirate your mother talks about."

His mother did not talk about her "pirate" except in private to Cuckoo; Volumna talked about him. It was Volumna who had told the tribe that Mellonia, having failed to be got with child in the Sacred Tree, had lain with one of the Trojan invaders—those same exiles who later had joined forces with King Latinus to rout the Volscians and the Rutulians and build the town of Lavinium to the north. Their leader was called Aeneas.

Cuckoo did not waste time in futile self-pity. It was a rare day when he was not ignored or bullied, and he had learned that hurt feelings need not keep him from practicing with his sling or planting pomegranate seeds in the garden under his mother's tree. Now he would pick some berries. Elderberries. His mother used them in pies and cookies. He knew of a patch beside that little river called the Numicus. . . .

At first he thought that the man was lying on his stomach and drinking from the stream. Cuckoo had never seen a true warrior, but he had heard so much about them from his mother—"valiant beings aglitter with armor"—and so much about them from Pomona—"killers and rapists, slyer than Fauns"—that he was stung by a beehive of curiosity.

Then he saw that the man was dead. He felt a shaft of unreasoning anger and unreasonable sorrow. To have found a warrior, only to find him dead! He could handle anger; it quickened his heart and gave him a surge of strength. But sorrow was something else, a dullness creeping down his limbs, a slow frost of lethargy. It was pictures too. . . . He saw a woman lamenting in a tent, her son beside her, and he had to remind himself that they were only the fancies of his mind. Still, he was sad for them, unbearably sad because their warrior would never come home to them.

He seized the man's feet and dragged him onto the bank and turned him on his back. A helmet, its tall plume wet from the stream but still nobly erect, hid the face except for the eyes, which were tightly closed. It was as if the face were locked in a prison. The helmet was bronze, with movable cheek pieces of leather. One of the pieces fell to the ground as Cuckoo freed the head, and he glimpsed a smooth cheek and gasped when he saw the whole face.

The man was very pale. He must have bled to death from the wound in his side (dagger wound, Cuckoo decided, too small and clean for a spear, but deep, deep). Except for his absolute stillness, however, he did not look dead, he looked peacefully asleep. His hair was silver like that of an old man. It made you think of the White Sleep. But the face was neither old nor young, it was ageless. The Dryads perhaps would not think him beautiful. Except for his mother, they did not think any man beautiful and they did not make images of their God. But Cuckoo saw what he would like to become (as if an ugly boy with streaked yellow hair could grow into a great warrior!).

He looked at the face for a long time and wondered what he should do with the man. If he left him beside the stream, the Dryads would weight him with stones and shove him into the water, or the Fauns would steal his armor, or the lions would eat his flesh. He must dig a grave. He had no shovel. The Centaurs had shovels but, while they were friendly enough in their superior way, he did not have time to visit their compound across the Wanderwood. He must use his hands.

The earth was relatively soft beside the river, which overflowed its banks when rains fell in the Apennines and left a rich soil riotous with clover and grass. He knelt and furiously began to scoop the earth, using a stick to dislodge an occasional stubborn stone. He was very tired when he had finished the grave. His hands

85

were raw and bleeding. He lay on his back and rested until he realized that he was resting not because he was tired but because he did not want to consign the warrior to the worms and his soul to Hades. Perhaps a funeral pyre ... Achilles ... Hector. ... His mother had told him about such heroes and how the quick fire had saved their bodies from the slow devouring earth. No, a fire might attract enemies.

He reached to his throat and removed the chalcedony amulet, shaped like a halcyon, and placed it around the man's neck as a gift for Charon. He knew that it was not particularly valuable, not like amber or carnelian, but he loved it and perhaps the gray ferryman, Charon, would measure his gift by what it cost the giver in love, not coins.

He wanted desperately to keep the helmet. But the warrior's friends might come looking for him, and he must leave the helmet on the bank as a marker for the grave, to show that the man had received a proper burial. Perhaps the helmet would be returned to the tent where the wife and son had grieved in his fantasy (those ridiculous fancies, how real they seemed!). The Fauns might get it, of course; he could frighten a single Faun with stones from his sling, but he was no match for a pack. He would wait until dark and hope for the warrior's friends.

He rolled the body, heavy with armor, into the grave. Momentarily and wonderfully the eyes flickered open and seemed to stare at him. Blue eyes. Halcyon-feather blue. It was only the motion of rolling which had opened them, however; when the body lay on its back in the narrow grave, they closed themselves as if in uneasy sleep. Then he began to gather violets. His mother loved them—she had placed them on the grave she had dug for his favorite drone, killed by the worker bees last fall—and he strewed them over the body and followed them with the freshly dug earth.

He did not know any prayers for the dead. All he could think to say was, "Mother Earth, receive him kindly." He slipped among the trees and climbed the slippery trunk of an elm to wait in its oval head of branches.

The sun sat high in the heavens like a great bronze

discus when he began his vigil. The sun was settling into the treetops when he heard and then saw the man walking along the bank of the river. Big man. Armorless. Loincloth and thong sandals, dagger at his side. And the face—he knew no words for the blue intensity of the eyes, the sunburst of hair which surely had never felt the bite of a comb. He thought of a phoenix. Once he had spied such a bird across the Tiber. It had leaped from the ground like a flame, leaving after it a single golden feather and an ache in Cuckoo's heart because *his* gold was ugly—everyone told him so—and he was bound to the earth and to the forest.

Was the man a friend or an enemy? From his face, he seemed to be walking in a dream, like one of the Dryads when she came from the Sacred Tree, except that he strode instead of glided, erect and proud, foot after foot with military precision. He almost stumbled over the helmet. He picked it up and brushed it clean of dirt and placed it on his head, and then quickly removed it and fell to his knees on the soft earth above the grave. Was he going to disinter the body? He might be an enemy after plunder. He had taken the helmet—he might want the rest of the armor too. Cuckoo fitted a stone in his sling.

He had never heard the tears of a man. He had heard the lament of the women when a friend was taken by a lion. A thin, high keening. He had heard his mother weep when she thought him sleeping on his lionskin couch, in their little beehive hut, high in their tree. But the sobs of a man—this man, at least—were like the bursting of one of those earthen dams built by the beavers, when the water booms its way into turbulent freedom. It was the weeping of a man who had probably not wept since childhood. Surely warriors were not supposed to weep! And yet his mother had said: "A real man is not ashamed to show what he feels. Achilles wept for his friend, Patroclus. Your father and his first son—your half-brother—embraced without shame in front of their warriors. True manliness is not being afraid that someone will take you for womanish."

The dam had burst, the flood escaped and subsided. Valorous among the violets, the man lay prone and spent above his silent friend. Cuckoo left his tree and

87

He had never heard the tears of a man.

walked toward him. It never occurred to him to exercise stealth; his big feet crunched in the leaves; anyway, the man was not listening for footsteps. He was not even aware of Cuckoo until the boy knelt beside him and touched his shoulder. The man jerked as if a hot brand, one of those bronze horrors used on slaves, had touched him, and sprang to his feet, looking down at the still kneeling boy like an angry Cyclops.

Cuckoo looked up at him, strangely without fear. "I buried your friend," he said. "I hope you don't mind. It was just that I didn't want the lions to get him. You see, they don't know any better."

Anger turned to puzzlement in the man's face. The blue eyes widened into a wounding pain. Finally he spoke, but with a deep rough music which Cuckoo had never heard in the measured eloquence of the Centaurs or the guttural grunts of the Fauns.

"You were kind to bury him."

"I didn't say a prayer. I didn't know one for a warrior."

"I'm not much for prayers myself. Besides, I don't think this man needs any."

"He was your friend?"

"He was my father."

Cuckoo knew what it meant to lose a father. "My mother taught me a poem," he faltered. "I'm not sure what it means, but it might be right for him. Shall I say it?"

"Yes."

> "Purple is distance:
> Hyacinth over the hill,
> Tyrian murex.
> Purple is distance only:
> Violets wilt in the hand."

The man did not speak or move. Was he displeased? The silence shrieked to be filled. "I hadn't much to give him as a gift for Charon. Only an amulet of chalcedony. It was shaped like a seabird."

Cuckoo had been kneeling until he had started to ache, and yet he was now afraid to rise—afraid for the first time—because he could not read the look in those blue and searching eyes. He did not need to rise. He was caught and engulfed and lifted as if by a sudden wave.

He thought: *I have buried his friend with the wrong poem and the wrong gift. He is going to sacrifice* me *to Charon.*

But the man did not kill him, he embraced him. Cuckoo had never been held by anyone except his mother. Were men supposed to embrace? The Fauns, yes, but they were not really men. Well, it was good not to be killed. It was good that someone wanted to hold him, big climsy boy that he was, though dwarfed beside this giant. He tried mightily to return the embrace, even though his ribs were about to crack, and he felt the man's cheek, not exactly bearded but with a few days' growth, rough against his face, and he smelled earth mingled with sea.

And then he heard his secret name:

"Halcyon."

CHAPTER II

Aeneas was dead, Ascanius wanted to die.

Had it come to this, that in the end there were no gods except the implacable, cruelly smiling Fortuna? That every battle, ultimately, was fought to be lost, that cities were built only to be burned, that heroes were born only to die like rustics and wander among the same eternal shadows?

The years stretched behind him like sea wrack straggling after an aged ship. . . .

The fall of Troy, the death of his mother in fire and carnage. The siren-voiced sea, luring the exiles with wind-beat and foam-burst, driving them with tempests and raking them along harsh coasts for fifteen years. The Lady of the Bees, so lately met, so early lost, like the drone she had loved. Defeat, exile, loss. But always, Aeneas—

The good times too, hope like a phoenix risen from its own ashes. The bounty of King Latinus, that wise old man, now dead, whose wisdom came from the woods, and who called Aeneas the son he had never sired.

"If you will help me to defeat my enemies, I will give you my warriors and half of my land, and my only daughter in marriage."

The wars with Turnus and his ill-trained but dogged Rutulians; Camilla, the Volscian, and her fleet-toed Amazons (and the sly Dryads who brought them spears carved in the Wanderwood). Aeneas triumphant in the grace of the gods. The building of Lavinium, the "second Troy." Small, yes, but built to grow. And always, in battle or banquet hall, his father beside him, ageless, dreaming, conquering Aeneas, poet and warrior; alway, Aeneas.

Until yesterday—

"There is a Faun at the gate."

"Has he come to beg?" Aeneas sat on a gypsum throne in the megaron. Logs made a tent of wood on the great central hearth, but spring was rich in the air with bergamot, warm with the unseen presence of Persephone, returned from the Underworld. Swallows had started to nest in the gabled roof. Woodpeckers hammered at round wooden columns.

"To ask your help, my king."

Aeneas liked the Fauns. He did not begrudge them their dirt and their lies. "Bring him to the hall."

Mischief knelt before him. He was very old; twelve years had been sixty to him.

"How may I help you?"

"Rutulians, King Aeneas, down from the north. Stealing our nets. Attacking our palisade."

"Many?"

"Few. But well-armed. And winter has made them restless."

"And us as well. We will find them for you."

The sword felt light in Ascanius' hands. Ares stirred in his blood. Enough of building; enough of waiting; enough of a winter with meager snows, little cold, but cold enough to keep the Rutulians in Ardea, the Dryads asleep in their trees, the Trojans in Lavinium.

They had found the marauders building a camp for the night. Tents like grounded birds, yearning for flight. Thorns heaping a fence against the lions. It was less a battle than a skirmish; mere boys, these Rutulians (Had *they* fought Achilles? They hardly knew his name!); no sooner met than routed, in the time it takes to lower a sail or hang a shield on the wall.

"Father!" Ascanius had called, lifting the visor of his helmet and searching among the men. "Father, we made quick work of them. We didn't even lose a man."

Euryalus' brother, the youth Meleagros, faced him, white with silence.

"Yes, Meleagros?"

"Your father—"

"Wounded?"

"Dead."

"How?"

"A knife in his side. I didn't see who struck him." Old eyes stared from his young face. He knew the meaning and meaninglessness of death. Euryalus and Nisus had died in the war with Turnus. Meleagros, then six, had seen their severed heads on stakes.

"His body?"

"Lost in the river."

It was almost night. They had no torches. They were close to the Wanderwood; it was foolish and useless to search in those Dryad-haunted fastnesses after dark.

"We must get the wounded back to the town. In the morning I will find him."

All night he had listened to the keening of the women as it rose into a shrill tumult, subsided into a low moan; Lavinia's voice louder than those of her attendants. Someone—was it Meleagros?—had brought him a potion of poppy-heads.

"It will make you sleep."

"Sleep is a little death. I have had enough of death."

Now it was dawn. The gray stone walls, the wooden megaron, the wattle huts, were flushed to a semblance of marble. He drew the thong which fastened the door to Lavinia's chamber in the women's hall. She lay on her jointed bedstead, her fleece of wool cast to the brick floor amidst tufts of hair shorn or pulled from her head. Her women crouched beside the bed like hounds around a wounded master. His eyes flickered over the room, avoiding the moment when they must fix upon Lavinia and he must somehow speak words of comfort instead of contempt. A three-legged stool. A chest of fragrant cedarwood. A soiled mantle hanging from a peg. A warp-weighted loom, woman-tall, and intricate with spindle and distaff and carded wool. A wicker basket resting on wheels and rainbowed with dressed yarns. Ascanius had never liked the room. He liked a

93

spear stand beside his door, a shield or a wolfskin on his wall. He had come here twice since the town had been built, and both times he had thought: *Lavinia hunches at her loom like a brick mason at his kiln. Mellonia's loom, I think, must move to her singing and spin wool into gold.*

Lavinia stared at him through tear-reddened eyes. It was hard to remember that twelve years ago she had been a shy, pretty maiden, desperately eager to marry the exiled Trojan leader who had fought Achilles and banqueted with Helen. Aeneas had not dared to refuse her. Refusal would have meant no alliance with Latinus, no friends in all of Italia, no Lavinium. He had pitied her; tried to love her; been unfailingly kind to her and never spoken of Mellonia except to his son.

"I am going to search for the body," he said then.

She did not speak; she looked at Ascanius as if in reproach because he did not wail and had not shorn his hair. It was true that his grief was locked in his blood like a frozen stream. He was one of those voiceless shades which are barred from crossing the Styx to wander eternally in the netherlands. Perhaps when he found his father's body, he would climb beside it on the pyre and his grief would find a tongue, even as the kindly flames embraced him with arms of oblivion and hurried his spirit after his father.

"And if you don't find it?"

"I will." How these Latin women thickened and coarsened with a few years! How dull they seemed with their kitchen talk, the price of wool or bread, a servant heavy with child by a man not her husband! Even their grief was that of an animal. He remembered Andromache bereft of Hector and hushed as marble; he remembered Mellonia when she had left his father. ("I am not one of those smooth, silken lilies. ... Not anymore. ...") Best not to think of her now, the Lady of the Bees, or of her son, his brother. Mischief had told him about the boy. ("Who does he look like?" ... "Aeneas.")

"You never liked me, Ascanius. And your father— he loved you best. Do you think I don't know? Do you think me stupid, you with your cold blue eyes and your

94

high Trojan ways? But I am carrying his child. You won't dare to harm me."

Even the flowers in the room, the wild roses and columbine, could not conceal her smell of sour goat's milk.

Gently he touched her shoulder. When one is dead, it is easy to be kind. "I never meant to harm you, Lavinia. Shall I send you a potion to help you sleep?"

"Go and find his body and give him proper burial."

The funeral pyre loomed like a shaggy thicket in the outer bailey, cedar piled upon elm upon beech; beside it, animals waited to be sacrificed, sheep and oxen, their fat to be used in swaddling the body before it was placed in the flames; and a copper urn to receive the ashes (there was little gold in this barbarous land).

How quickly Lavinium dwindled behind him! Lurked, that was the word for the wretched town, set on two hills in the midst of a clearing but still afraid of the forest. The second Troy? A village built by children, it seemed to him now. Children who had remembered the Lion Gate at Mycenae, the unbreachable walls of Troy, but had wrought in a strange land with puny materials, wood and wattle, small gray rocks instead of cyclopean stones. Its low hills, known as the Twin Turtles, where circled by walls no taller than two spear lengths. The outer bailey was cluttered with canvas stalls and round huts which had scarcely left room for the funeral pyre; the inner fortress was splendid with one gabled megaron, but otherwise humble with workshop and stable, vegetable garden and women's hall. The second Troy? The ghost of Troy. ("That city you mean to build. It may not be the one. . . .")

It was a time for ghosts.

"You mustn't go alone, Ascanius," said the guard at the gate, a quick little man with eyes which could see in the dark. He was called the Cat by those who remembered the multi-colored cats, imported from Egypt, which had lounged beside the lotus pools of Troy. The conquering Hellenes had slaughtered the cats along with their masters.

"I must," he said.

He was not to be left alone. Who was that ancient figure creaking toward him across the field? A moving tree stump . . . an ancient Faun.

"King Ascanius." It was Mischief.

He wanted to strike the fellow. *(It is true, though; I am now the king in place of my father.)*

"I am to blame," Mischief faltered. "It was I who called him forth—"

The fellow had doubtless come to ingratiate himself with the new king. Perhaps, too, he had come out of some faint compassion, lodged like a bit of amber in the dirt of his calculating heart.

"No, Mischief. It was valor which called him forth. You were only a messenger."

"Shall I come with you to look for his body?"

"No."

He had followed the river Numicus from the point of the battle, from the scuffed earth and the litter of a half-built and quickly forsaken camp, of fallen tents and scattered thorns. He was hardly aware when the trees took on the look of figures shrouded for a funeral; when woods became Wanderwood; when a place to hunt became a place to hide.

His eyes glanced dully along the surface of the stream, and momentarily he looked for a snow-haired man playing with a dolphin, but other snows had taken the man, and the dolphin, if age and the Tritons had not destroyed him, swam in other waters, and who could play fetch and carry in a world which had died for the second time?

He almost stumbled over his father's helmet. The violets, the fresh-packed earth—someone had come here ahead of him. There was no need for the funeral pyre in Lavinium.

Grief burst in him like an ice-locked river struck by the early spring sun, and he fell, stricken, onto the grave, his fingers clawing the sand.

"Halcyon."

"How did you know my name?" the boy asked.

"You just told me about your gift to Charon. A

halcyon bird. It was a good gift. It seemed a good name for you."

"Oh," said the boy, disappointed. "I didn't think I said what kind of bird it was. I thought perhaps— But of course that's how you knew. Nobody ever calls me Halcyon except my mother. The others call me Cuckoo."

"You don't at all remind me of a cuckoo. I would have said a halcyon."

The boy looked as if he thought that Ascanius might be ridiculing him. Eyes too large for the thin face, serious, blue as the lost Aegean which washed the coasts of Troy.

"But a halcyon is swift and beautiful."

"I know. I imagine with those long legs you can outrun a deer." He touched the boy's hair. "Where did you get such hair?" It would not be right—it would be a terrible wrong—to say, "I am your lost brother, but it isn't safe for us to meet again. Volumna will harm your mother if she finds us together."

"I got it from my father, I expect. He was a great warrior. A bit of a pirate too, but he only plundered from wicked folk."

"And your mother is a Dryad. I can tell from your ears. Is she young?"

"Rather old, I would say. Close to thirty. But very beautiful. The Fauns call her the Lady of the Bees. She looks as if she were spun out of honey. I didn't take after either parent."

"I would say you took after both of them." Spun out of honey . . . his father had made such phrases.

"You don't have to be kind. I know how ugly I am. I really don't mind. This way, the Wanderwooders leave me alone."

"Do you like to be alone?"

"I like to be with people I love. But there's only my mother. Not that she isn't enough. It's just that we need a man in the tree too. To teach me things. My mother taught me to read. About Achilles and Hector and Ajax—and of course Aeneas. How to tell a good mushroom from a poisonous one. What kinds of flowers have feelings, though I never learned to hear them. 'But I can't teach you how to notch an arrow,' she said,

97

'or build a boat, or hammer a helmet out of bronze. Those are a man's skills.' "

His green tunic fell above his knees, his sandals of antelope hide clung precariously to his feet; there was a sling thrust in his sash, and a pouch of stones hung at his side. It was true that he had grown too fast. He was mostly legs and arms, with narrow chest and shoulders, but his face was strong and, with a little more weight and a smile, would become handsome. With the edge of his tunic Ascanius brushed the dirt from his father's helmet until it shone like a bronze mirror.

"Look at your reflection."

"I don't like to."

"Look! What do you see?"

"Neither this nor that, and not much of anything."

"Nonsense. You've been listening to the Dryads. Do you think I am ugly? I have yellow hair."

"It looks good on you. But mine has that funny silver streak, and it never stays in place."

"Does mine stay in place?"

"No. But it looks as if it were meant to wander."

"Why not allow yours the same liberty?"

"The Dryads say that neatness is one of Rumina's first laws."

"There is also a goddess named Aphrodite."

"Venus? We aren't supposed to worship her."

"You'd better. Anyway, I think she would like your hair." He almost said: "As she liked your grandfather's." "Besides, I like it. I have to go now, Cuckoo." Indeed, he must go before he stole the boy to Lavinium (and risked the Dryad-half of his life, taking him from his tree), or at least claimed him as brother.

"Oh, no," cried Cuckoo with desperation. "We've just met. I want to hear about your battles. How many princesses you've saved." *How like my father,* Ascanius thought. *I would have asked: "How many men have you killed?"*

"But I must tell my friends about finding my father and how he was properly buried."

"Of course," sighed the boy. "I don't suppose you could come back again? Or I could come to visit you in your city? It must be Lavinium. That's where the warriors live, with King Aeneas."

98

"I've heard about your queen, Volumna. She doesn't like warriors. She would be very angry if she knew you were meeting me."

"Nobody cares what I do except my mother, and she tells me to be a man and do what I like. I think Volumna would be delighted if a lion ate me, though I manage to get along with them. I know I would be delighted if a lion ate *her*." (*A bit like me as well as my father!* Ascanius thought.) "When I was small I put a mole under her tree to gnaw the roots. She had shamed my mother before the whole council by calling her a man-lover."

"What did the mole do?"

"She killed it after the first nip. She thought it came on its own. Now she has a moleskin rug in her tree."

"Perhaps we *could* meet again."

"Tomorrow!"

"The same time?"

"I'll already be here when you come. But I don't even know your name."

"My real name is secret like yours. Think of a name for me by tomorrow." He bent and hugged him without even wondering if the sons of Dryads liked to be hugged by strange, tall warriors. The thin arms squeezed him in return.

"Tell your mother that I think she has a son to be proud of."

"I will tell her I met a god. Are you? My mother says Apollo has golden hair."

"I knew a god once. I'm not even fit to speak his name."

"You mean your father, I expect. I thought that about him too. But there are different kinds of gods."

"I'm not any kind at all."

"I think," said Cuckoo, "that what makes a god is people to worship him. Even one person, if he worships enough."

Ascanius surprised himself with a laugh. The boy was so intense and serious, like a philosopher propounding a new concept of the world. That it was round instead of flat. That there were five elements instead of four. Never once had he smiled.

"I'm a pirate at heart, that's what I am."

99

"Pirates sometimes make better friends than gods. You can talk to them, you don't have to pray. Remember me when you select your next crew."

"I think you would make a fine helmsman. You notice things."

"I have a lot to learn about pillaging, though."

"Practice some more on Volumna's tree. Good-bye, Halcyon." He watched the thin, angular figure disappear among the greenery with a backward look and a wave and his first tentative smile. He thought with astonishment: *For one little moment I have forgotten to grieve. I am like a sailor who has lost his ship in a storm but found a dolphin.*

CHAPTER III

He found the Dryad oaks as murmurous and excited as a giant beehive; in fact, the little hives under the trees mirrored in small the activity of the circle. Unlike Fauns or Centaurs, the Dryads rarely lost their Olympian grace. They walked or they ran but in either case they almost seemed to glide, their feet scarcely touching the earth, their arms aflutter behind them like trailing wings. Now they were not in the least graceful, they were frenzied, but not, it would seem, with fear. His mother had told him that they had such a look when they armed Camilla and her Amazons to fight Aeneas. ("As if they were hungry," she had said, "and a feast of broiled partridges awaited them.")

Volumna looked over or through him; she was never concerned with a boy whose father had been a man. Now he was less than nothing to her. The other Dryads skirted him as if he were a weed or an ant nest. Except Segeta, who acknowledged him with a distant smile.

"Go to your mother," she said in her deep chthonian voice, but before he could ask for an explanation she had trailed after Volumna like a wisp of smoke.

Thank Jupiter for Pomona, who refused to be hurried at any time!

"Have the lions left the Wanderwood?" he cried to her.

"Oh no, it's something much better. We're going to the council chamber to celebrate." Rarely had she looked so opulent; there was an amber ripeness about her, and perhaps it was time for her, however young, to visit the Tree.

Something better. Her "better" was likely to be his worse. No where did he see his mother. Was she going to be driven out of the circle?

"What is it?" He must ask the question though he dreaded the answer.

"Aeneas is dead. Mischief brought us the news," she called over her shoulder, even as she joined the general exodus, undulating after her elders and followed in turn by a swarm of bees which somehow looked like wasps.

For a moment he did not associate Aeneas with the warrior he had buried beside the Numicus. He felt a dart-sting of grief, but a remote, impersonal grief for someone he had admired but never met, a great hero who had fought Achilles and later settled in Italia to build Lavinium, which he had never seen and which, built by Trojans, seemed almost as distant as Troy to a boy who had never left the Wanderwood.

"Stabbed in the gut," said Pomona as a happy after-thought. He would have liked to send a stone whistling into *her* gut. The thought surprised but did not shame him. He was expected to be either insignificant or disreputable, and it was more fun to be disreputable.

Then it struck him, chilled him, enveloped him like a shower of ice shaken from a wintry tree. The man he had buried had been Aeneas, the son of a goddess. Had he not thought of him as a slain god?

He climbed the narrow, carved steps in the trunk of his mother's tree and stepped into the hive-like house, its myriad round windows open to the spring air and bespeckled with bees. He had left his mother sitting at her loom.

He found her seated on a three-legged stool and holding a papyrus scroll, half unrolled, in her lap. From its yellowed, much-fingered edges, he recognized the eyewitness account of the Trojan War. She was not reading the scroll, however; she might have been carved from wood. Pale-barked beech. Her green hair, spilling over her shoulders, accentuated her pallor. She did not look at him. He remembered that Aeneas had been her favorite Trojan warrior—even above Hector—and she had wanted Troy to win the war. ("Hector could fight

102

and love, but Aeneas could dream too. He was a bard as well as a warrior and husband.")

He knelt beside her stool. "You're not going to the council, Mother?"

Volumna demanded attendance from all of her Dryads, except in case of oak blight or another illness, which affected the dweller as well as her tree.

"No, Halcyon."

"Volumna will be angry."

"When has she not been angry?"

"Mother, it's very sad that Aeneas is dead." He put his arm around her shoulder and wondered if he should tell her about the burial, how he had spoken her poem and included a gift for Charon; later, perhaps.

"He would not have wanted to die in such a way," she said.

"He was a great warrior. He should have died in a great battle."

"I don't mean that at all, Halcyon. He never cared about glory. It's just that there was so much work for him to do."

"But something good has happened too."

She looked at him with a lostness which seemed to say: "What good thing can ever happen at such a time?" He was almost afraid to share his news.

"I have found a friend. . . ." She was trying to listen; she was squeezing his hand with quiet urgency. But her voice was dim and funereal, as if it were coming from beneath a pile of brown, decaying leaves.

"He wouldn't tell me his name, but I think he's Aeneas' son."

Quickly he told her about the meeting on the bank of the river, and then she made him repeat his story, dwelling on every detail. How did he know the man's identity? What was the color of his hair and eyes? Had he seemed kind without being soft?

"And I'm to meet him in the morning. You must come too."

They left their tree when the blue-eyed owls had ceased their nocturnal hootings and dawn was an intimation of pink on the horizon. There were no sounds in the Dryad trees, no voices, neither stirrings of coal in braziers used for frying pheasant eggs, nor sighing of looms and supple fingers. The hives lay hushed as deserted tree stumps; woodpeckers had not begun their tiny depredations. The Dryads were sleeping heavily after their meeting in the council chamber. Doubtless they had made a festival of the occasion. Their singing had been audible even from the Ficus Ruminalis, half a mile from the circle. Dryads professed to abhor the orgies of the Fauns, but at their own festivals they drained many a sheepskin of potent elderberry wine, aged in casks among the roots, and more than one Dryad had lost her way returning to her tree and run afoul of a Faun and borne his child. Mellonia was the first Dryad in the Wanderwood to bear a child by a mortal instead of the God, but such incidents had become more frequent since her shame, as Volumna unfailingly reminded her, and there were even rumors that several Dryads had yielded willingly to odorous, shaggy lovers.

Now they sat and waited beside the Numicus, silent, shrouded by elderberry bushes as tall as three warriors standing on each other's shoulders, and white with dense oval flowers which, in summer, would cluster with tiny black berries. A dragonfly poised above the stream, whose meanderings made a small sweet music of water and rock and root. Never once did his mother take her eyes from the bank and the prints left in the grass by the sandals of the stranger. She clung tightly to Cuckoo's hand, and he realized with a quiet pride—he was not often proud and the feeling was good—that he was both larger and stronger than his mother (she who had been the unshakable strength which had sustained him in an otherwise loveless life) and able to give protection as well as company. One thing he knew but dared not ask. She had known Aeneas as more than one of the uncountable heroes in a scroll about a distant war; known him as a friend. Perhaps she had been to Lavinium. Perhaps . . . ?

"Someone is coming," she said. He heard the rustling stream, and a dove in a cypress tree, mourning to its mate, and then, as his heart leaped like a netted quail, the tread of sandals in grass.

104

"He isn't wearing armor," his mother said. "His step is too light. He forgets the danger."

Then they saw him. Yes, it was his new friend, Aeneas' son. Ascanius he was called. Cuckoo had learned the name from Pomona, who had learned from the Fauns. ("Aeneas and that lecherous son of his," Pomona had said with fascination. "Two of a kind, killers and rapists.")

Yesterday Ascanius had seemed to walk in a dream of sorrow; today there was an aliveness about him; anticipation tempered with wariness. He was watching for enemies but he seemed about to smile. *It is I, Cuckoo, who have made him glad,* thought the boy. *There must be something about me which no one except my mother has ever seen. Something more than ugliness and awkwardness, than untidy hair and out-sized legs. Something to love, even for one as great as the son of a great king.*

He rose from the grass and the warrior smiled to him as to a comrade-in-arms.

"Mother, this is my friend," he began. She too had risen from her concealment; now she waited; and Cuckoo saw her for the first time as a woman as well as his mother, no longer simple and simply loving him, but with a heart as secret and labyrinthine as the forest; sunlight and shadows, concealment and grassy glades. A woman capable of loving others besides her son, and in ways beyond his comprehension. When had he really looked at her? She had been a presence to be accepted, not examined. Protective and comforting. Yesterday when he had said that she looked like spun honey, it was only because he was asked to describe and made to remember and reach for words. Now he saw her reflected in a stranger's eyes. Ascanius, the golden and god-like, stared at her as if she were a goddess.

Indeed, she was worshipful. Her green tunic was bordered with purple hyacinths. Her necklace was strung with malachite sea gulls. Her sandals were fastened with buckles of ancient green copper. Except for her choice of a sea instead of a forest bird, her dress was much like that of the other Dryads, but there was a difference about her which lay in a pride which was not haughty, in a strength which was not hard, in a sadness

105

which was not self-pity. She was a hyacinth like those embroidered on her tunic. Protected by bees. Petals for her friends. Stingers for her enemies. There was no one like her in all of the Wanderwood.

But her newness was also strangeness, and strangeness threatened to become estrangement. An eloquent stillness seemed to envelop her and Ascanius and exclude Cuckoo. Would they never move or speak or remember that he was with them? *They have forgotten me, he thought, and it was I who brought them here to meet at the river. My own mother and my new friend.* It was as if he had found a treasure on the beach, a casket of amber and coral from the sea-cove of a Nereid, only to lose it to a sudden wave.

They seemed to yearn toward each other without quite touching, without knowing how or if to touch. At last Ascanius fell to his knees and pressed his head, his cornucopia-golden hair, against Mellonia's knees, and she drew him to his feet and kissed him on the cheek and Cuckoo knew and wondered how long he had known without quite knowing, without presuming to know, that he, pathetic, ugly Cuckoo was the son of a great warrior and king, and Ascanius was his own half brother.

In the light of such knowledge, it was worse now to be excluded from the embrace. What was the good of a brother who yesterday had hugged him and today ignored him? Of a mother who had loved only him and his nameless, unseen father for eleven years and now forsaken him for a stranger? He thought: *If I vanish into the woods, perhaps they will think that a lion has eaten me and be ashamed of their neglect.*

But it was he who was ashamed. He had underestimated both himself and them. Almost with the same motion they reached out to him and drew him into the magic of their arms, their intimacy. No circle of Dryad oaks could ever bring such a wonder of warmth even to the Dryads, even to proud, confident Volumna. Thus, in this time of loss, of finding his father only to find him dead, he had found more than he had lost. His brother loved him. His mother had drawn him more richly into her love.

They sat on the river bank, Ascanius between his

mother and him, but not dividing them, an arm around each of them, and silence was not a wall but an open gate, a communion more intimate than any speech.

Then, small words held large meanings.

"The long years have forgotten you, Mellonia. You're still a girl with green hair, watching beside a river."

"They have remembered you. You have grown more like him."

"He would have been proud of his son."

"And so am I. Does Lavinia know about him?"

"No."

"Was she kind to your father?"

"Yes, in her way."

"What is she like?"

"A wineskin emptied of wine. A purse without coins. But harmless enough."

"Ascanius, you never liked women much, did you?"

"Oh, I've had a woman or two in my time."

"Desired. Possessed. I said liked."

Ascanius looked perplexed and stared into the stream as if he hoped to find the answer in its meandering currents, its speaking stones.

"Mother, you shouldn't ask him such a thing," cried Cuckoo. He had not meant to speak. It had seemed a time to listen, and indeed he had learned astonishing things. But his mother's question sounded like an accusation.

"It's all right, Cuckoo. Your mother can ask me anything she likes. Perhaps she's right. With two exceptions."

She did not press him to give their names. "Did your father love Lavinia?"

"How could he, after you and my mother? He liked her. He found her—comfortable."

"She was what he needed, a coverlet against the frost."

"But you were a fire."

"Small warmth to him, I'm afraid. Or you either. Volumna hates you, Phoenix. As much as ever. You still can't come to my tree, nor Halcyon and I to Lavinium."

"Then we shall meet here."

107

"We're still in the Wanderwood. The Fauns have long ears. The grass tells secrets. Nothing has changed except that I have a son and you have lost your father."

"No," he cried. "We can't have lost him for nothing. It isn't like him, even in death, to be so cruel. We will find a way to meet, the three of us."

She touched a finger to his lips. "Hush, my dear. I must listen."

"I don't hear a thing."

"Trust to my keener ears. You can't hear the grass complain or the daisies shriek." She rose to her feet. "Someone is coming. You must go now, Phoenix."

"When can we come here again?"

"I don't know. Never, unless you go!"

"What do you hear?"

"The grass cries out—a Dryad. Several. On both sides of the river."

"Close?"

"Too close. Run as if Achilles were charging you in his chariot!"

"And leave you, Mellonia?"

"They won't hurt me. You they will kill. And perhaps my son. You must take him with you."

"I won't leave my mother," Cuckoo said stoutly. "They'll shut her in her tree and steal her bees."

Ascanius seized his shoulders. "Cuckoo, there are several ways to be brave. The brave thing now is to run. Trust your mother and me. I'll get you back to her."

Cuckoo trusted him. He kissed his mother's cheek. "We'll both come back." Then, to his brother:

"We can't follow the river. It's the easiest way and exactly what they expect. They'll head us off. Nobody can outrun a Dryad."

"Do you know a better way?"

They left the river, the dragonfly, the elderberry bushes, and entered a part of the forest so dark that the sun was a dim constellation in the night of foliage above them.

"The Dryads don't like it here," Cuckoo said.

"Because it's so dark?"

"Yes. And there is no grass, and there is lion-scent

everywhere. They will falter and hesitate and look around them before each step." The trees in that scarce light looked gnarled and ancient. Oaks mostly; occasional beech or elm. Saturn's trees, they were called. Once they had been blithe saplings, but now they were wrinkled and gaunt and bitter, with sorrow as well as time. When Saturn left the land, they had locked their branches against the sun and killed the grass at their feet. The Dryads did not like them.

A lion stood athwart their path, so still that he might have been one of those sculptured beasts of the famous gates of Mycenae (Cuckoo had heard about them from his mother). A male, newly grown to his full strength, and huge, huge, to a boy. Cuckoo tasted a hemlock of fear in his mouth. He had never met this particular lion.

But he gripped Ascanius' hand and said, "Don't worry. They're used to me."

"You aren't afraid of lions?" Ascanius gasped. "It takes a Hercules to kill one."

"It's a question of choices. The Dryads are worse right now. Besides, the lions prefer female meat. Less stringy. And it isn't their time to feed."

Nevertheless, Ascanius reached for his knife.

"Put that away. You'll make him nervous." Then, to the beast: "Friend of Saturn, may we pass?"

Saturn's friend looked at them with the lordly pride of one who knows himself master in his own part of the forest. Mischief twinkled wickedly in his eyes. Lions were as individual as Dryads or warriors in their appearance. *This one,* thought Cuckoo, *is playful, fond of fun. Curious too. He has seen Dryads, Fauns, Centaurs, but never a skinny boy like me, whose yellow hair is streaked with silver. His appetite is prodigious, and in spite of what I told my brother, he is hardly one to wait on a particular time to feed. He is deciding if he will maul us, eat us, or welcome us.*

Cuckoo advanced with more confidence than he felt —the boom of his heart might set the beast upon him— and stroked the tawny mane. *(I will pretend that he is a Centaur. I will pretend that he is Bounder, my mother's friend, who died before I was born.)*

He was careful not to stroke against the grain. The

109

"Put that away. You'll make him nervous."

hair was moss-smooth beneath his touch. The great head twisted on the powerful shoulders and leaned to Cuckoo's hand.

A rumble came from the throat: "You can pass. Indeed, I will escort you," it seemed to say.

The friend of Saturn trotted docilely beside them until they reached the edge of the forest, paused for a final caress, watched them benevolently as they climbed a small hill and disappeared from his sight and country.

A meadow stretched below them, daisied and green, hillocked by huge ant nests, and islanded by the twin turtles of Lavinium. It was the first real city which Cuckoo had ever seen.

"We don't need to worry now," said Cuckoo. "The Dryads won't follow us out of the trees. I expect they won't even get past our friend, who may just change his eating time. Even if they do, they fear Lavinium, and no wonder. It's a great city."

"One day perhaps," said Ascanius. "Not yet. Not like Troy. But it will give us shelter."

He stared at Cuckoo as if to study him. "Have you ever stayed for long away from your tree?"

"For two whole days I was lost in the woods."

"How did you feel?"

"Tired, hungry, and thirsty, though I found mushrooms to eat and a stream to drink from. I've never stayed longer than that."

"But now—"

"Half of me is like you, isn't it? I expect I can learn to live without my tree. At least until we can find a way to help my mother."

"Cuckoo, you're brave like your father."

"No one ever told me that except my mother."

"Now you have a brother to tell you."

"Mothers and brothers are prejudiced, aren't they?"

"Yes, but not in this case."

"I think the best thing is to kill Volumna. But that presents a problem. She's very durable. It takes more than a hungry mole."

"You know, Cuckoo, I think there's a bit of me in you too."

"Do you? I hope it grows."

111

Arm in arm they crossed the meadow and climbed the ramp to the town. Every few steps Cuckoo paused to gasp, "But this is a *great* city. No enemy could topple those walls."

"You should have seen the Hellenes with their catapults."

"But the gate. Why, it's made of bronze. Like a huge shield."

"The Hellenes had battering rams. Cedar trunks with bronze heads."

"Well, there aren't any Hellenes here." They *would* save his mother. He and the king of such a proud, strong city. He and his new brother. Ascanius would think of a plan which would do credit to wily Odysseus. After all, Ascanius' father—*his* father too—and Odysseus had fought in the same war.

But Cuckoo was very tired. There was so much stone in the town, so little wood.

CHAPTER IV

There was little time to think about Mellonia and how she had seemed to come to him out of yesterday and not his youth, the girl with green hair and the endless blunt questions, a very old child, a very young woman, unchanged except that she looked as if she never expected to meet another Bounder, another Bonus Eventus, another Aeneas. What she had lost was neither wonder nor beauty, but expectation.

There was only time to think about Cuckoo.

Behind the central hearth, a wooden staircase rose to the second floor and the gallery where Ascanius slept in a little room with a pivot-hung door and a polished spearstand and a jointed bedstead. He had lost track of the times he had climbed those stairs, sturdy as stone, cedar-fragrant, for Cuckoo lay in the bed, desperately ill, and Ascanius had acted as priest and physician, nurse and brother to him. He had brought him a blood pudding, roasted in the paunch of a sheep, from the central hearth. But Cuckoo had not been able to swallow a single bite. He had brought him flagons of wine sweetened with honey and cylices of goat's milk, but Cuckoo had either vomited or lost consciousness after a few sips. He had brought him woolen fleeces to warm him during his chills, and sponges to cool him in his fever, and he had sat on the bed beside him and listened when he talked about his mother or asked about his father. It seemed that all sicknesses were converging on him, a host of malignant demons intent on his destruction, and nobody knew the cure, not even the physician priest, Alkaios, a brown little man with a springy step which made him resemble a cricket and which made Ascanius detest him for seeming so unconcerned at such a sorrowful time.

It was the fifth day, and the worst, which Cuckoo had spent away from his oak in the Wanderwood. It might be the last. The illness had begun on the second day. On the third, Ascanius had wanted to invade the Dryad circle with his warriors and return the boy to his tree. Cuckoo had quickly dissuaded him.

"They'll hear you coming and burn the tree. They'll get Mother too." His voice was thin and tired, but it carried a quiet authority. Never once had he whined or complained.

"How can I help you, Cuckoo?"

"In Mother's scroll about the Trojan War, there's a god named Paion who healed the Olympians when they were wounded."

"I've already offered him six sheep and twelve white cocks. What about local gods?"

"There's always Rumina, but that's Volumna's goddess. No hope there. We'll just have to wait."

Ascanius' and Cuckoo's grandmother, Aphrodite, was the goddess of love, not health, but on the chance that she might know the proper god for such an illness and intercede in behalf of her two grandsons—the sick one and the worried one—he offered a tiny prayer:

"Grandmother, I don't often go to your shrine and I've never fallen in love except once, but don't hold my omissions against Cuckoo. He's a good boy—like his father. Help him and I'll do anything you ask of me. Even get married."

No one except Alkaios, who had learned his skills in Troy, had been allowed in the room. Alkaios, and the youth Meleagros, he who had told him about the death of Aeneas in the skirmish with the Rutulians. Meleagros was a slim, small boy who played a lyre as if he were a Faun and, too slight to wield a sword, handled a dagger with the agility of a Trojan cutpurse. In one of his fitful wakings, Cuckoo had said:

"My mother sings to me when I'm sick. Will you sing, Ascanius? Something sad. But not *too* sad."

"My voice sounds like a toadfrog. But I know someone who can sing like a nightingale and play the lyre too."

Meleagros had worshiped Aeneas. He brought his lyre and came to Cuckoo's bed and looked at the boy with tenderness and awe and with the look of one who had lost his own brother, Euryalus, and understood what Ascanius stood to lose.

"Will you sing for him?" Ascanius asked.

Meleagros sang:

> "Catch the blue dolphin
> Of the morning in your net.
> At night unbind him;
> Loosen his silken burning
> For the luckless fisherboys."

"It's still morning for us," Meleagros hurried to add, "with a lot of dolphins to catch. Maybe we can catch some together."

Cuckoo gave him a wan smile. "Thank you, Meleagros. When I'm well, will you teach me how to use a dagger? I want to hit a knot hole in a tree at fifty paces. Volumna's tree."

"If you teach me how to live in the woods. Find food. Catch fish and animals."

"With the fish you use a net. With the animals, you have to know which are enemies and which are friends. Vipers and weasels make good stew. Never trap a mole. Make friends with a lion or else keep out of his way."

"What about bears?"

Cuckoo closed his eyes.

"Come back later, Meleagros," Ascanius said. "Your song did him good, I think."

It had cheered but not strengthened him. He continued to ebb, to lose color and weight, like a tree as it sheds its leaves and shrinks before the coming of winter.

Ascanius was not good at waiting. He made unnecessary trips up and down the stairs, carrying everything from food to coverlets to bowls of water, sacrificing sheep and cocks between climbs (chasing away Alkaios with a curt, "I'll do it myself. I know more about the gods than you do.").

115

Now, on the fifth day, there was nothing to do except wait, and he felt as spent as Cuckoo, who lay pale and diminished on the bed, between sleeping and waking, coverlet thrown to his feet, his bones showing through his blue flesh. Ascanius himself had hardly slept in five days. He sat on the side of the bed holding Cuckoo's hand and imperceptibly stretched full-length beside him and fell into a demon-haunted sleep, even as he heard the occasional bray of an ass in the outer bailey, the scuff of boots as the menials went about their tasks of fetching wood to the great hearth in the hall, the nervous murmur of men who had lost their king and gathered below the window to wait for word about the king's son.

He seemed to be clambering from a pit of dry autumn leaves. He kept reaching for roots to find a handhold but clutching leaves which crumbled at his touch and left him no nearer the top, where a muffled voice was speaking words which he could not understand. Finally, hand over agonizing hand, he clawed his way up the earthen walls and out of sleep. Then he saw who it was who was talking.

Lavinia sat on the opposite side of the bed. She held a cup in the shape of a ram's head and she was lifting Cuckoo's head with her free hand and coaxing him to drink.

"This will help you, Cuckoo."

"I can't keep it down."

"Try. It's something new. It will give you strength."

"Who are you?"

"Someone who wants very much for you to be well."

Cuckoo began to drink.

Anger engulfed Ascanius like a shower of sparks from a wind-blown fire. That Lavinia or any other woman should come unbidden to the men's quarters—that she should come now, with Cuckoo at the point of death—it was worse than impudent, it was unforgivable. And what was the green bubbling liquid in the cup?

She is poisoning him, he thought. *She wants her unborn son by Aeneas to become the king of Lavinium after me. Not Cuckoo. Not Mellonia's son.*

He struggled to his feet, still drugged with too little

116

sleep too quickly broken, and circled the bed to strike the cup from her hand. She looked up at him with neither surprise nor fright in her large, bovine eyes. They were not, however, the eyes of a poisoner.

Still, she had no right to be in the room and feeding his brother some primitive and no doubt worthless medicine. Herbs picked in the light of a sickle moon? Blood of a sheep sacrificed to the infernal goddess, Furrina?

She did not turn from his gaze, nor lower the cup from Cuckoo's lips. She looked as if she expected a blow or, at best, an order to leave the room, but meant to return at the first chance and renew her ministrations. She looked stupidly but inflexibly stubborn.

Cuckoo had drained the cup.

"What is it, Lavinia? What have you given him? He'll only vomit it, you know."

"Green acorns," she said. "Crushed in elderberry wine. You forget I am a forest woman myself." Her late father's capital, now ruled by her brother, was little more than a village on the other side of the Wanderwood; his "country" an area of town and fields, farmhouses and forest hardly larger than the territory once encompassed by the walls of Troy. "When I was a child I played with a Dryad girl. Her mother gave her such a drink when she had a fever, and she was quickly cured."

"His fever comes from being away from his tree. Chills, hunger, thirst as well—you don't think crushed acorns are going to save him?"

"Acorns—and his father," she said.

"My father's spirit?" he cried. Spirits admitted to Hades could not, even if they wished, return to haunt or help the living, except in a waking vision or a sleeping dream.

"His blood," she said. "Half of the child is human. And his courage. Any other boy would have died by the third or fourth day."

It was true. Most grown men would have died if they had been as sick as Cuckoo. Not only had he not complained, he had even tried to keep Ascanius from worrying about him.

Ascanius sat on the bed beside Lavinia. It was a long

time before he spoke. "I don't think anything will help. I don't even think he can keep it in his stomach. But you meant to help and it was kind of you. And you know who he is, don't you?"

"Of course I know. Do you think I would want him to die because he was my husband's son by another woman? I've always known about Mellonia. The Fauns tell me things just as they do you. The one called Mischief is full of tales. I've envied Mellonia all these years. The last woman your father loved. But I've never hated her. He was a god. Any woman he chose must have deserved him. I didn't even as a girl. I lacked that delicacy he looked for in women. But I'm not going to hurt her son. I'm going to help him if I can."

He looked at her with surprise. It was true that her eyes were large and round and lusterless—gray or brown? It was hard to say—but they were not blank and not, he decided, stupid. The pale, freckled skin, the shapeless body, the sagging breasts, the overlarge hips. Was there not a comfort in the very plainness of her? Though a queen, she made no demands, of admiration or obedience. What he had thought stupidity was a lack of learning. She did not know how to read; she spoke Latin and no other tongue. But learning was not wisdom. He had never troubled himself with either loving or hating her. Only with mildly disliking her. ("You don't much like women, do you?" Mellonia had asked him.) He took her hand and pressed the pudgy, calloused fingers. She had always occupied herself in the women's quarters, more like a servant than a queen, though Aeneas had begged her to let her attendants do the work. Weaving, cooking, baking wheaten bread, pounding clothes on rocks in the river Numicus before it entered the Wanderwood, scouring a table with fuller's earth—always busy, always being herself, a plain forest woman who had won the man she loved, but not his love. A once comely girl who had lost her youth, but wasted no time with kohl or carmine, jewels or empurpled gowns; gone about her work as wife and woman and, when it was demanded of her—when people came to her to cure their children or console them for a bad crop or a lost child—a queen. "You and your

118

high Trojan ways," she had accused him. Her own ways were humble but they were not low.

Cuckoo was sleeping a deep and untroubled sleep. He had not vomited the potion. Ascanius and Lavinia watched over him, silent and side by side on the bed; and he kept her hand and thought: *Seven days ago she lost her husband. I lost my father but found my brother and Mellonia. Till Cuckoo fell sick, my grief was solaced and shared and made endurable. Who has comforted Lavinia except a few ignorant women (but perhaps like her they are less ignorant than I have supposed)?*

Cuckoo opened his eyes when the sinking sun seemed to perch like a phoenix in the one square window.

"I'd like some more of that wine," he said.

Ascanius looked at Lavinia.

"Have you any more?" he asked. She pointed to a crane-necked vessel at the foot of the bed.

"Will you fill his cup?" he asked.

This time Cuckoo was able to hold the cup between his hands and drain it in a few gulps.

"It's very good," he said. "Now we must start thinking about Mother."

Ascanius held him in his arms, his little brother, and thought that he felt him shake with a chill, and held him more tightly in order to give him warmth.

"Don't cry," Cuckoo was saying, "I'm not going to die," and Ascanius knew that it was he who was shaking, not Cuckoo, but he was not ashamed, even before Lavinia. He turned to smile at her, to thank her.

But Lavinia had left the room. Her big frame, her rough, rawhide sandals, had made no sound on the red and blue tiles of the floor.

"Who was the lady who brought me the wine?"

"That was Lavinia."

"My father's widow? But she was dressed like a serving woman, not a queen. That plain brown robe without any border of flowers. I rather thought that queens wore purple robes. Dyed with the murex shell."

"She always dresses that way."

"Never mind. She doesn't need purple. She's very beautiful, isn't she?"

CHAPTER V

Ascanius and Cuckoo waited impatiently in the hollow oak of Ruminus. The smell of leaves was rich in the air; the bright afternoon sun yellowly rimmed the door. Cuckoo was still a little weak, but much too strong to remain in Lavinium while his mother was held a prisoner in her own tree, and he was growing stronger with the excitement of their mission, his own importance, indeed, necessity, in a plan to rescue his mother and humble Volumna. Ascanius' men waited at the edge of the Wanderwood. They must not be seen; they must not be heard by the grass or spied by Mischief and revealed to the Dryads. If necessary, they could be summoned by a blast on a Triton shell.

Cuckoo had led Ascanius, unobserved, to the tree by skirting those meadows where the Dryads liked to languish in the sun, those coverlets of grass which cried with pain if a sandal bruised them.

Now they awaited the arrival of Pomona, who had been announcing for several weeks, loudly and frequently to every Dryad in the circle, to passing Fauns and Centaurs outside the circle, to Mischief and even to Cuckoo, the day and the time when she was going to visit the Tree. ("Aren't you afraid of Sylvanus?" Cuckoo had asked her before the death of Aeneas, before he had met Ascanius. "My mother is a queen," the girl had replied. "Ruminus will hardly allow that wrinkled old dwarf to take God's place.")

"What if she doesn't come?" Ascanius asked, fidgeting among the leaves, apprehensive like most men of action when they must scheme instead of fight.

"She'll come," said Cuckoo with certainty. Three days ago, he had lain at the point of death; today, he was flushed with confidence in his brother, in himself, and in a plan which he himself had devised. Ascanius had explained to him how the Fauns assaulted the Dryads in the Tree; how none of the Dryads except Volumna and Mellonia knew the secret.

Cuckoo had not been surprised. "I never liked the God. I'm glad he doesn't exist. And since he doesn't, we can use the Tree ourselves. To kidnap Pomona."

"If she comes."

"Pomona is ready for *something*. If there weren't a Tree, I expect she would trap a Faun on her own. Then she would claim he had sprung upon her out of a thicket and taken his pleasure." (Ascanius had carefully explained to him the facts of sex, and Cuckoo, far from being shocked, had commented delightedly, "Our grandmother was very clever to think up such a thing. No wonder men worship her. How long must I wait?")

Mischief was easily bribed into keeping the other Fauns away from the Tree. "A suit of armor now. If the plan succeeds, a lyre, a flute, and a drum. You can be your own army."

Pomona did not disappoint them. They heard her bidding good-bye to Volumna, who had escorted her to the edge of the field. They could not hear what she said to her mother while she drank the opiate, not even Cuckoo with his pointed ears, but they heard the trill in her voice, the confidence, the anticipation, as she left her mother to meet the God. She might have been going to a harvest festival, the kind which ends with an orgy. They heard her crossing the field and humming a song, rather like bees buzzing around a fig tree (or wasps?).

They crouched in the shadows against the barky walls between wooden protuberances as she flung open the door, then closed it carefully behind her, and settled herself in the leaves, patting them into a bed, removing her jewels—anklets, necklace, bee-tipped pins—and wriggling out of her tunic, like a snake out of its skin, to luxuriate in her nudity. The sun outside the tree had dazzled her eyes; otherwise, she might have seen them. She might have screamed before Volumna was out of earshot. At length she did see them, Ascanius at least.

"Are you the God?" she asked, anticipatory. "All I can see is a tall, splendid outline." He stepped toward her. She struggled to rise from the leaves and languished into his arms. The drug had started to work. She was pleasant to touch, soft, round, and ripe. He was not a girl-lover, but Pomona's body, whatever the limitations of her mind, was that of a young woman. His purpose denied his desire, but he could not help thinking, *What a waste, what an infernal waste for all those Dryads to deny themselves to my men. Perhaps things will change—*

"Well, are you?" she repeated. Dryad princesses, it seemed, were not awed by gods.

"No, there isn't any god. I'm Aeneas' son, Ascanius, and I've just taken you prisoner. You are not to scream, or I will have to throttle you."

"Ascanius?" she yelped, more with pleased excitement than fear. "The rapist. Are you going to take me?"

"Yes, back to Lavinium."

"What will you do with me there?"

"We shall have a long conversation."

"Is that what you call it? You realize my ignorance of such matters. I'm not surprised, though, about the God. The old ones take things on faith. But my friends and I have wondered for some time exactly what went on in the Tree. We've even envied our shameful sisters to the north who make love in the fields. After all, who wants to be got with child in her sleep? And who's that with you, Ascanius? I see someone else in the shadows."

"Cuckoo," answered Cuckoo.

"You're much too young for this sort of thing. Or are you? You seem to have grown a great deal lately. Well, no matter. I always rather fancied you, Cuckoo, though Mother punished me whenever I said I didn't think you were ugly. Just clumsy. She called you Aeneas' whelp." Her speech had begun to slow and slur. "The boys we expose with their pointed ears. Who but a . . . Faun could be their father? As for myself, I prefer a human,

122

whatever my mother says. Now that you've told me, Ascanius . . . I wish you would be about your business before I fall asleep. It's all very well to bear a child . . . but it seems a shame to miss the *getting*. Must we wait for Lavinium?"

"Yes."

"Perhaps it's just as well. Then I'll have time to wake up . . . and do things properly in a bed instead of these prickly leaves."

"You don't understand. You're to be my hostage, not my wench." Somewhat desperately he tried to re-unite her with her tunic. She was not in the least helpful. In her feeble way she actually seemed to be thrusting the garment away from her. Merciful Zeus, would the potion never silence her?

"Not even once?" she sighed.

"No."

She subsided nakedly into his arms, unconscious at last, whether from the drug or disappointment it was hard to say.

"I'll go after Volumna," said Cuckoo. That too had been his own plan. Ascanius had wanted to bring Me-leagros with him to run the perilous errand. "But I know the woods," Cuckoo had argued. "And the Dryads won't dare hurt me. Not when I tell them you have Volumna's daughter."

Ascanius lifted the girl in his arms, her tunic scarcely covering her thighs (she wore no undergarments, im-modest girl!), and carried her out of the Tree. He paused to watch the long-legged boy as he loped across the meadow, avoiding the daisies; he followed him in the eye of his mind through the woods and to the circle of oaks, to Volumna's tree, and finally to the tree where Mellonia waited a sad eternity for news of her son.

Volumna entered the hall more like a conquering queen than a bereaved mother. Her upswept hair flick-ered with malachites and amethysts (which of them tipped with deadly points?). Her sandals of antelope leather slapped the blue tiles with precise taps. An emerald bee twinkled between her breasts with no visi-ble support. Though shorter than any human woman in the hall—than the kinswomen of Lavinia, who stared at her with indignation and envy—she gave the illusion of height; she shimmered as she walked, and with manner as well as jewels. Only her silvering hair hinted at her incredible age—three hundred and how many years? In truth a queen.

But Ascanius was not awed. He remembered Hecuba, he remembered Helen. He sat on the gypsum seat of his griffin-flanked throne; a purple mantle clasped his shoulders; his crown of chrysolites burned less brightly than his extravagance of yellow hair. He did not like the throne or the pomp or the crown; he did not like to sit where his father had sat. But he liked watching Volumna cross the room in front of his warriors, assembled along the walls, and in front of Cuckoo and Lavinia, seated on smaller thrones to either side of him.

Pomona sat on a three-legged stool at his feet. Meleagros had been assigned to guard her. She had stopped talking to him only when her mother entered the room, and she had been talking with more animation than one would expect from a girl whose cheeks had lost their customary flush. It was her second day from her tree.

Volumna acknowledged her daughter with a quick, reassuring smile, but the smile became a stare when she faced Ascanius.

"Kneel," said Ascanius.

Volumna did not so much as bow her head.

"Kneel, you bitch, before I carry you up those stairs and play the Faun. Has Medusa turned you to stone?"

Volumna knelt with hurried dignity.

"Greet my brother and my father's widow."

Cuckoo did not wait for a greeting. "Is my mother all right? Have you taken her food and drink?"

"Wine and partridges, acorns and pheasant," Volumna said. "She has eaten better than when you foraged for her."

"I doubt it," said Cuckoo. "And you haven't knelt to my stepmother yet."

Volumna repeated her obeisance. "Lavinia, as a woman and queen, I appeal to you, who are also a woman and queen. Is it fitting that I be humbled before your husband's son by another woman? The Volscian queen, Camilla, was my friend. You and I could also be friends."

Lavinia, ill at ease in a tight lavender robe and looking as if she would prefer a kitchen to a hall, suddenly became the queen Volumna had called her.

"Your friend Camilla warred against my husband. And you sent her spears. I would sooner befriend a Jumper."

"Thus the amenities," said Ascanius. "Now the business at hand. You have something I want, Volumna. Mellonia's freedom to leave her tree. To leave the Wanderwood, if she chooses, and visit Lavinium with her son, whom I have named my heir. In turn, I have something you want. Your daughter. It seems to me a fair exchange."

Volumna's speech was unhurried but not quite so commanding as that time, twelve years ago in the forest, when she had accosted Ascanius with his father as they left the Tree. When she met his gaze, she blinked as if she were looking into the sun, though the room was lit only by the great hearth, where lambs were turning on spits, and by the light from clerestory windows.

"Mellonia is not in danger. It is true that she is a captive in her tree, but her sins have been unspeakable. I forgave her long ago when she lay with your father, but when she met you beside the Numicus, she forfeited forever my good opinion."

"We talked, nothing more."

"No matter. She knew what she was about. She broke her promise to me."

"Forgive her again."

"I cannot think you would harm my child, whatever you feel toward me. You are Aeneas' son. Was he not vaunted for his compassion?"

"I am Aeneas' son," said Ascanius, "but I understand that you called him a butcher. Anyone will tell you that I lack my father's heart. If he were a butcher, I am a Cyclops. No, I would not harm your daughter. I would simply allow her to die for want of her tree. After my men and I have taken their pleasure with her."

Once, with his father, he had noticed her resemblance to a Jumper. She still looked as if she would like to spit venom at him.

125

"I like it here, Mother," Pomona hurried to say. "They have been kind to me, especially this nice young man, Meleagros. But I am a little tired. I miss our tree." The succulence had drained from her cheeks. She was like a fig assailed by bees.

Volumna spoke with effort. "Very well, Mellonia will have her freedom."

Ascanius did not try to hide his skepticism; indeed, he flaunted it like the head of an enemy on a pike. "But will she keep it, once we return Pomona? I never had reason to trust you in anything except your unreasoning hatred for men."

"You have my word. I swear by Rumina, the nursing mother, that—"

"Your word and your goddess are worth about as much to me as the mud on the banks of the Tiber. Only your daughter has worth for me now. I intend to keep her until I have proof of your promises. She is losing her color, it is true, but I hardly think she will die before the third or fourth day. This is what I intend to do. I will have her held in the palace. Fed, tended, treated as a guest, not a prisoner, even as you see her now. Meanwhile, I will lead my best men—some fifty or so of my seasoned warriors—to your council chamber. There you will assemble your Dryads—there you will not be able to call down your bees upon us—and you will tell your friends about the Tree . . . your lies . . . the Fauns. Perhaps when they hear the truth, they will find it propitious to choose a new queen. One who will treat Mellonia and her son as they deserve. If not, I shall make the choice for them and dispose of a certain ancient tree in your circle of oaks. As for making promises which you later intend to break, I should tell you I lack my father's compunction about destroying your tribe. Aeneas spared them because Mellonia thought them her friends. But none except Segeta has proven so. It may be their fear of you has made them ignore Mellonia. At any rate her life has been lonely and friendless for twelve years, and also that of her son, my brother."

"As you wish," she said. "I will summon the council for the hour before dusk."

Ascanius turned to Cuckoo and Lavinia. "Has the

126

queen of the Dryads your permission to depart from this hall?"

"You are a wicked woman," said Cuckoo. "Remember the mole that gnawed at your roots when I was a little boy? I sent it there myself. You can go now, but if you hurt my mother, I'll send something worse."

When she left the hall, Lavinia muttered to Ascanius. "I don't trust her. Her eyes seem hooded even when they are opened wide."

"I know," he said, "but I don't intend to be bitten."

Ascanius was considerably less confident than one would have guessed from his straight carriage and stern visage—anyone except Cuckoo, who always seemed to know how he felt. But Cuckoo was safe in Lavinium, notwithstanding his insistent requests to accompany his brother. "Guard Pomona," Ascanius had said to him. "Get Lavinia to feed her that acorn drink. It won't save her—she hasn't a human father like you. But it may prolong her, and we certainly don't want her to die on our hands."

He had stationed men at the entrance to the council chamber to examine the entering Dryads and to divest them of poison pins or other weapons. He was guarded in the chamber by armored men—some twenty-five of his best—with swords and shields, greaves and cuirasses. But Volumna was as treacherous as a Faun, and far more cunning, and the cool, impassive faces of her friends did not inspire confidence.

Still, she made her confession without evasions, with the dry, clipped tones of an army scout: the destruction of her tribe by the lions; the death of her mother the following year; her trust in a Faun who had befriended only to ravish her; the truth about the Tree.

"I did not want you to know so painful a truth," she concluded. "I wanted to spare you my own knowledge and the awareness of your own humiliation. I do not ask your approval. I only ask that you do not judge me." The one movement in all that room was the flickering shadows cast by the olive oil lamps and the open brazier which supplied the coals to light them. The one sound was the hushed breathing of Dryads whose thoughts were as unreadable as their faces, the

127

somewhat louder breathing of brave but fearful men who did not wish to seem cowardly in front of the women who hated them.

Ascanius could not read the faces of the Dryads, those white petals against an earthen night. But then he had never been very good at reading a woman's face, even in the light of the sun. A man could look stern or fearless or sad. It was very hard for him to look inscrutable. A woman, however, looked as she chose, and among her choices was the inscrutability of a Sybil.

No children had come to the council, only the young girls and mature women, those who had visited or were about to visit the Tree. *It is hard for them,* Ascanius mused, trying to imitate his father's sage and careful deliberations. *It is hard for them to learn in so short a time that their enemies have been their lovers, their god is a myth, and their queen, for whatever reasons, a liar.*

He looked from face to face and tried to pity them and surprised himself by noticing that they were not, after all, identical in their impassivity, but individual, each feeling and hiding the revelation in her own way. Segeta was not Volumna; she was cool but not cold, frost but not snow. Rusina—was that the name of the Dryad with ears as tiny as hawkmoths?—was staring from him to Volumna with a ghost of pain. Perhaps there was hope for them. Perhaps they would willingly choose a queen in place of Volumna and the Wanderwood need no longer be a menace for men, and Dryads and warriors could talk and perhaps—who could say?—make love. (Aphrodite knew that most of the women in Lavinium were plain, pathetic things; elderly Trojans, weathered by hostile seas; their daughters, who had not flourished in this alien land; and the kinswomen of Lavinia who, like her, inclined to grow stout or squat after the flush of youth.)

It was Segeta who spoke, and she seemed to confirm his hope. "But, Volumna, shouldn't we have been allowed to choose? We have been used by the Fauns. We have exposed our sons to the lions. We have done a cruel thing to Mellonia and her son."

"I spared you the pain of choice. It is a queen's prerogative and also at times her anguish."

128

"But now we have no choice. Not even you. Not with your daughter held in Lavinium."

In the light of those twinkling lamps, it seemed to Ascanius that a tragic resolution had come into Volumna's face. There was a kind of greatness about her. So far it had been for evil. But now—?

She lifted her arms as if to exhort her people to pray to the Nursing Mother.

"There is always a choice, if only in the way we die." The life seemed to drain from her face, as though she had been too long away from her tree. Muffled in silence and weariness, she fell to her knees. He almost pitied her. She seemed about to faint.

There was, however, another door to the room, lodged in the dirt floor—a circle of wood on leather hinges, which she was raising like the lid on a wine cask. He in turn raised his sword.

"Volumna, my men will kill you if you try to leave this chamber."

"But it is my own chamber," she smiled. "It is you who will leave to make room for my friends."

Horror was entering the place. A hundred horrors. Jumpers. An insidious black tide, they flowed from the pit, from the catacombs of the earth, the labyrinth which led to Hades. A black tide, flowing as if to the exhortation of the moon, slow, rhythmical, inexorable. He had anticipated an assault by bees; he had disarmed the Dryads of their poisonous pins. But the poisoners themselves, beloved of the Dryads, obedient to them, pets to them as cats had been pets to the unconquered Trojans—only his father could have foreseen and forestalled such a threat.

Doubtless there was considerable poison left in the mandibles which flashed amberly in the light of the lamps—clicked like dry twigs brushed by the wind. There was even a lethal beauty about them, this force as natural as lava, obeying laws beyond Ascanius' knowledge, deadly to those who tried to arrest them, but not consciously evil. Not like those who directed them.

The room seemed to die. It was the light which died, the lamps extinguished in quick succession, in quick

*"It is you who will leave to make room
for my friends."*

little breaths from the Dryads closest to them; the brazier covered with a copper lid. In the dying light, he had only time to read astonishment in most of the assembled faces. For once, they had not had time to compose their features into impassive masks. He did not doubt that Volumna had carefully planned the attack, had led the Jumpers from their nest beneath her own tree, but she had not dared, it would seem, to make all of the Dryads her confederates. Only those whose loyalty she could know to be unquestionable even after her revelation about the Fauns. Still, it was doubtful comfort that most of the Dryads were unprepared for Volumna's treachery. They remained her subjects. They remained the masters of the advancing tide which rustled over the dry leaves with the ominously innocuous sound of raindrops.

Now he could only see the green eyes which shone with their own fire. The black tide had become a starry night. Beautiful, beautiful and deadly. Soon to expand about his feet with innumerable individual deaths. He was the king, he was Aeneas' son. He must speak or act to save his men.

Speak first, then act—hard for this man of action. "Volumna, you will let your daughter die?"

"Yes, Ascanius. And the men you left in Lavinium can come and destroy our trees. But you will be dead. You and the men in this room, and many of those who come to avenge you."

Some of the Dryads had started to whistle with sweet piping notes like those of a mistress to her pet. The tide was dividing, separating; the Jumpers were moving among his men.

It was the eyes which saved him from the first attack. They paused and fixed upon him. He could hear the clacking mandibles. Sightless, he could visualize in the dark the eight contracting legs, hooked and hairy; the concentration for the fatal jump. He had sidestepped spears, he had ducked javelins. Now he sidestepped a deadlier weapon; he spun his body with the grace of a warrior who as a child had watched Achilles; as a boy, had fought beside his father. He felt the brush of those writhing legs; heard the thud of the body in the leaves beyond him, turned and savagely trod with his

131

sandal where he had heard the sound, and felt the muscular body twitch into death even through the leather sole.

His voice reverberated like a struck shield. "Dryads, your queen has said that there is always a choice. You can choose life. You can choose the fathers of your children. You know the Fauns to be odorous savages. You think my men to be savage. But have they approached your queen in cruelty or treachery?"

Silence extinguished the room. Silence which was to sound as black was to color. Nothing remained to say; only to act.

He could not hack at the dark with his sword; he would strike his friends along with the Dryads. He could only tread on those eight-legged deaths, aim at the eyes, the chill, unblinking eyes which they could not hide. Perhaps he would die; most of his men would die. *Cuckoo will grow into a wise king. But Mellonia, what of her? Cursed with almost-immortality. Locked perpetually in her tree, the White Sleep yielding to green spring (but not for her); the years becoming generations (but not for her). My father was right. His love was doom.*

There, and there, in answer to the low sweet hums, the horrors continued to move, to circle his men, to circle him. . . . He raised his shield against a second assault and felt a thud against the sharp-ridged bronze.

"We have had enough lies." Cool Segeta spoke with fire. "Why should we die for the foolish pride of a hard old woman? She who would sacrifice her daughter and us as well? Help me to light the lamps."

The dying coals of the brazier, freed to the air, leaped into orange. Segeta lifted a coal between tiny copper prongs. *"Help me to light the lamps."*

The walls trembled into brown earth and friendly roots, and each lamp shone like a separate moon. The night was losing its deadly stars.

"Hush, hush," Segeta was saying, driving the Jumpers back into their nest, and others joined her in the sweet keening whistle of exorcism. It was as if the earth were reasserting its supremacy over the Underworld, life over death.

"We will choose a new queen, Ascanius."

132

CHAPTER VI

Cuckoo loped through the woods toward Lavinium. His long legs sped so lightly over elm leaf and grape vine, root and stone, that he hardly felt them beneath his sandals. He felt—strong, agile, important. Important with his mission. He was carrying a message from his mother to Ascanius: "The Dryads will come to pay fealty to you when the chariot-sun bestrides the sky." Three days ago she had stepped from the prison of her tree as if she were rising from the White Sleep, pale and tremulous. Today Cuckoo had left her as radiant as when the storks returned from Libya and her tree had burgeoned with buds and nests.

Ascanius had not waited to greet her; he had hurried directly from the council chamber to Lavinium to release Pomona. No one had seen Volumna since she had been deposed as queen. She had not returned to her tree, even to greet her daughter.

Cuckoo began to whistle as he reached the bank of the Numicus. Abruptly he stopped; perhaps he ought to grieve above his father's grave.

"Father," he whispered, "is it well with you in Elysium?" He had heard of the dead returning in dreams to console the ones they had loved, and indeed he could hear a voice. Was it the trees, rustling with woodpecker beat and swallow wing? Was it his father's ghost or the conjurings of his own mind? "Do not grieve for me in this happy time when Trojan and Dryad have learned

133

to live at peace. When Mellonia and Ascanius can meet as friends, and you are one with them."

The next sound he heard was decidedly not in his mind. Leaves were parted, earth was trodden, lightly, carefully, and yet by a large shape. Lion rustle, what else? He started to cross the river and hasten his steps. It was not a time to risk an encounter with an unfamiliar and possibly foraging lion. But there was something familiar about the rustle, the scent of fur and earth. No two lions were the same in movement or scent. It was Saturn's friend, the same animal who had befriended him and Ascanius when they had met Mellonia beside his father's grave. It would be unthinkable not to exchange a greeting.

Between two beeches, among elderberries, a narrow path dwindled into the deep darknesses of Saturn's woods.

"Cuckoo."

Volumna stood in his path, athwart his path. Her torn gown bristled with cockleburrs. Her hair tumbled, unfilleted, over her ears, and the silver had almost effaced the green, snow enveloping grass. She looked like a very old woman; she looked her three hundred and how many years.

She had lifted a blowgun almost to her lips, a small delicate weapon hammered from silver and disarmingly like a flute. With the least motion, mouth would touch mouth; with the least breath, death would fly to his face, his heart, wherever she chose to aim. Her aim was formidable; she had been known to hit a woodpecker on the wing at fifty paces. He could charge; he could run; he could not escape her darts.

"I've been waiting for you," she said. "You're going to Lavinium?"

"Yes."

"To join your brother. Aeneas' other son."

"Yes, Volumna."

"There is something I want you to know." She looked so white and old that for one incredible instant he thought: *She is going to ask me to intercede for her with my brother.*

"Your father died in a skirmish with the Rutulians."

"I know."

"It was I who saw them in the woods. They had come to hunt, no more. But I said to Mischief, 'They have raided your nets. Attacked your camp. Killed some of your friends. You must tell Aeneas. He will rout them for you.' Mischief believed me and did as he was told. I did not even have to bribe him."

"And my father came and the Rutulians killed him—"

"He came, but it was not the Rutulians who killed him. Did you really think those pathetic, ragged warriors could fell the hero of Troy? He was battling three of them at once and more than holding his own. Shields were splintering before his famous sword. One man had fallen to his knees. Another had turned to flee. Aeneas' back was turned to the undergrowth, the bushes, the trees. It was I who stabbed him. No one ever saw me. No one sees a Dryad in her leaf-green tunic when she does not wish to be seen. To Rutulians and Trojans alike, I was leaves and mist and nothing more. *It was I who killed your father.*"

He was no longer afraid of her darts. Eleven years of anger consumed him like a thunderbolt from Zeus. He was a tree enkindled by the heavens with holy fire. Unlike a tree, he could move, charge, attack her in spite of her weapon, in spite of the darts and their rapid poison. He could outleap a Jumper.

He was still too slow. Something moved ahead of him, another and deadlier lightning out of the woods of Saturn. Sharp-eared Volumna had forgotten the first lesson of the forest: Never forget to listen.

"Friend," cried Cuckoo. "Don't swallow her whole! You'll poison yourself with her darts!"

The warning was unnecessary. Saturn's friend was much too fastidious to risk a stomachache. With the nicety of a cook preparing a fowl for a king's banquet, he had plucked her clean of such small, indigestible impediments as cloth, pins, and darts. Now he was taking his leisure with the feast.

The forest was coming to meet the plain. Led by their new queen—and even Cuckoo did not yet know whom they had chosen—the Dryads were coming to swear obedience to Ascanius, king and conqueror. They had woven narcissus blossoms into their hair; they were

135

carrying baskets heaped with pomegranates like red gold. It might have been a festival, it might have been a funeral. Perhaps it was both.

Ascanius and Cuckoo waited for them at the head of the ramp which ascended from the field to the town. The field was festive with Fauns and Centaurs, who had gathered from the furthest reaches of the Wanderwood to watch the hated Dryads humbled before the Trojans. The Centaurs, always the agriculturalists, had mushroomed the field with stalls—round wooden planks beneath blue canvases—where they hoped to sell their vegetables, their lentils and gourds and squashes. The Fauns had not come to work, only to watch the confrontation, and possibly to steal what was left unsold or unwatched. Cuckoo sniffed the air, which was redolent of stale fish as well as fresh fruit, and spotted Mischief, remarkably spry, poised with helmet and breastplate and also carrying a flute, and looking as if he were equally prepared to attack a city or play a tune.

Inside the city, most of the populace, some three hundred men, women, and children, had lined the walls to greet the Dryads; all except those who were guarding the ramp, or the person of the king and his brother and Lavinia, for even now Ascanius did not entirely trust the Dryads.

"For all we know, the new queen may be worse than Volumna."

"Pomona is too young to be queen," Cuckoo reassured him.

The procession undulated out of the forest like a great green serpent, and Cuckoo had to look closely to see the separate tunics and remember that the Dryads did not always act in unison. He had grown up with them but he still envisioned a Dryad as one who obeyed her queen without question, rather like a worker bee, and even at the sacrifice of her own identity. He sometimes forgot that there were also Dryads like his mother, who did not in the least resemble her former queen; and that the new queen would exact a different kind of obedience and project a different ideal. His sharp nostrils caught the scent of bergamot, though Ascanius protested that the air reeked of fish ("Those

136

filthy Fauns," he muttered.). Everyone could hear the song of the Dryads, plaintive and plangent ("only night heals again") but joyful too ("the birds will build in the boughs").

"Are they happy or sad?" Ascanius asked. "I can't tell."

"Neither can I. Even after eleven years. They don't seem to know themselves. Will Segeta be their new queen?"

"I would think so," said Ascanius. "After her speech in the council chamber. She was the only one who had the courage to speak against Volumna. But it's hard to tell. All of them are wearing narcissus, but no one is wearing a crown."

"Phoenix, let's go to meet them. I don't care if you are the king. There's my mother, and she's smiling to us."

"All right, Cuckoo. But don't run. We have to keep some dignity for the sake of our men."

The two brothers descended the ramp, Cuckoo leading the way and trying to walk at a dignified pace, but his mother was so woundingly beautiful—he had never seen such ruddy cheeks—why, they outshone the pomegranates in her basket—that he began to run, and Ascanius kept up with him, and then he was in his mother's arms. How frail she felt, how small! How wonderfully strong and protective he felt, he who had led her to Ascanius and at last to Lavinium!

He did not forget his brother. "You hug her too, Phoenix."

Ascanius hugged her until Cuckoo tapped his shoulder and whispered, "Ask her who the new queen is."

Ascanius released her and blinked and stammered and said with a shyness rare for him, "We have prepared a f-feast for you, Mellonia. But where is your queen? It's only fitting that I greet her."

"You already have," she laughed. "In a very unregal way!"

"But you're so young," Ascanius cried. (Young? thought Cuckoo. At twenty-nine!) "And you aren't even wearing a crown."

"I waited for you to crown me. You are lord of the forest now."

He removed his crown of chrysolites and placed it tenderly on her head. It was large for her, but the jewels could not outshine the malachite green of her hair.

She in turn presented him with her basket of pomegranates. "A small gift but given with love."

While Ascanius stared at her as if she were the first woman and certainly the first queen he had ever seen, Cuckoo watched the Dryads and tried to guess their thoughts. No longer did they seem cool or smug or impassive. Oh, it was true that some of the older ones still had a certain arrogance about them. Submission to men? Unthinkable! They stared stonily ahead of them and you would have thought that he and Ascanius were slaves or Fauns, and that Volumna and not his mother was leading them. But Segeta, Rusina, and most of the younger Dryads simply looked divided between hope and doubt (except Pomona, who had spied Meleagros on the wall and was looking at him with little doubt and much hope). Would Mellonia be allowed to rule or would Ascanius rule for her? Were the Dryads to be subjects or allies? All their lives—and some of their lives ran into centuries—they had been told that men were brutish savages. But now a man had crowned their queen with his own crown, and his men were watching them from the walls with anything but savage looks, with a wistful yearning which would have softened the heart of a Gorgon.

Ascanius addressed the Dryads with outward composure, though Cuckoo suspected that he would rather be confronting a horde of charging Hellenes:

"I have prepared a feast for you and your queen in the city. I ask you to come as my honored guests and greet my men, who have sailed from a distant land. We lost our city to fire and pillage; we lost most of our ships to a hostile sea. We have never felt at home in these strange forests, locked up in our city. It is for you, as well as us, to unbar gates."

Mellonia answered for her people. Cuckoo was baffled and proud at the same time. It was hard to accept his mother as a queen. But a light had come into her eyes. As if she had seen—or remembered—a god. She made him want to kneel to her.

"We too have felt the burden of bars. All the more cruel because we lived without walls and thought ourselves free. But the truest freedom consists of letting in, not keeping out. It is a time for unbarring gates."

Mellonia between them, Cuckoo and Ascanius ascended into the city—the queen, the prince, and the king. That other queen, Lavinia, watched them from the gate, and Ascanius bowed to her and Mellonia smiled, as if to say: "You too loved Aeneas. We will not forget."

"I wish my father were alive," said Ascanius. "He would have been so proud—"

"I remember something he told me," said Mellonia. "About Dido. How she tried to turn summer back into spring, and ignored the drip of the water clock, the shadow of a sundial. Do you remember, Ascanius?"

"Yes."

"I think it's a greater mistake to turn summer into fall, and listen too intently to the water clock, or fix your eyes on the shadow."

"You're speaking in riddles," said Ascanius. "Like my father."

"You know exactly what she means," said Cuckoo.

"I'm not sure. What I want her to mean is too much to hope."

"Phoenix," she said. "Do you hear anything?"

"Why, yes, I do. The sound of wings."

"A swallow perhaps? A woodpecker?"

"No. A dragonfly."

Author's Note

Please don't blame me for making Carthage contemporary with Troy, blame Vergil, who was a better poet than historian. I am greatly indebted to him for the general, unhistorical background of my story, though the love affair of Aeneas and Mellonia is sheer invention. Mellonia, incidentally, reappears as the heroine of my story *Where is the Bird of Fire?*, becomes the beloved of Remus, and makes good her promise to help in the building of a "second Troy."

I apologize to the shade of Dido for my unflattering portrait of her. She is one of my favorite queens (doomed, beautiful women are irresistible to me, as to Edgar Allen Poe); however, I have shown her through the eyes of Ascanius and I felt that he would have resented and reviled her for trying to replace his mother.

The poems quoted in the story are my own and they are reprinted with the permission of *The North Carolina Quarterly* and *Cornucopia*. The phrase "Only Night Heals Again" is borrowed from a poem by H. D. which, incidentally, also gave me my title *Where is the Bird of Fire?*

DAW PRESENTS MICHAEL CONEY

Theodore Sturgeon wrote of Coney that "it is heartening to see a good writer become very good."

☐ **RAX.** The coming of the cold sun meant the ending of their world . . . or such it seemed. A truly different novel!
(#UY1205—$1.25)

☐ **THE JAWS THAT BITE, THE CLAWS THAT CATCH.** A symphony of sharks, bondswomen, and a social crisis in times to come.
(#UY1163—$1.25)

☐ **THE HERO OF DOWNWAYS.** Though they cloned for courage, it took more than breeding to find the light.
(#UQ1070—95¢)

☐ **MONITOR FOUND IN ORBIT.** An outstanding collection of the best stories of this rising light of science fiction.
(#UQ1132—95¢)

☐ **FRIENDS COME IN BOXES.** The epic story of one deathless day in 2256 A.D.
(#UQ1056—95¢)

☐ **MIRROR IMAGE.** They could be either your most beloved object or your living nightmare!
(#UQ1031—95¢)

DAW BOOKS are represented by the publishers of Signet and Mentor Books, THE NEW AMERICAN LIBRARY, INC.

DAW PRESENTS THOMAS BURNETT SWANN

An utterly unique writer of fantasies and imaginative legendry. . . .

☐ **GREEN PHOENIX.** A tour de force of the final stronghold of the prehumans of the Wanderwood and of their strange defense against the last legion of fallen Troy.
(#UY1222—$1.25)

☐ **HOW ARE THE MIGHTY FALLEN.** A fantasy-historical tapestry of a queen of ancient Judea who was more than human, her son who became legend, and the Cyclopean nemesis whose name became synonymous with colossus.
(#Q1100—95¢)

☐ **THE NOT-WORLD.** The story of a strange balloon flight that brought three English venturers into an older and .more enchanted land to mingle their fates with the last of the weird folk.
(#UY1158—$1.25)

DAW BOOKS are represented by the publishers of Signet and Mentor Books, THE NEW AMERICAN LIBRARY, INC.
